Daniel Driver Thomas

Poems of Adelphia

Daniel Driver Thomas

Poems of Adelphia

ISBN/EAN: 9783337408046

Printed in Europe, USA, Canada, Australia, Japan

Cover: Foto ©Andreas Hilbeck / pixelio.de

More available books at **www.hansebooks.com**

POEMS OF ADELPHIA

BY

DANIEL DRIVER THOMAS

ADA, OHIO
THE UNIVERSITY HERALD PRESS
1897

TO MY WIFE,

WHO, THO' IN THE CRUCIBLE OF
AFFLICTION, WAS WILLING TO LEND A HELPING HAND,
AND BY WHOSE ENCOURAGEMENT MY LABORS
HAVE SUCCEEDED THUS FAR,
THIS VOLUME
IS AFFECTIONATELY DEDICATED
BY THE AUTHOR.

CONTENTS.

PREFACE.

In presenting this little volume to the public, it is the author's design that nothing shall be degrading; if possible, the reverse. Had the author sought his own comfort, it is certain it would not have appeared to be taken up by the critic, or, which is worse, to be passed by in ominous silence. It was a pleasure to write the lines which came usually unbidden and were always welcome, and now at the request of friends they are published.

Some of the verses were written in younger days when looking to "connubial felicity." These may not appear best to those of maturer years, but it should be remembered that the moral sentiment has not been forgotten.

There has been no attempt at arrangement, but like the tho'ts themselves, they have been set down as they happened to come. Many thanks are due the printers for their patience manifested while the book was in press, and to all who have kindly aided in bringing the work before the public.

D. D. T.

Williamstown, Ohio, December 20, 1897.

Poems of Adelphia

Theodosia.

THE wailing winds my fancy hears anon
    Whene'er I muse on that I muse to-day.
It is a tale of direst woe and gloom
    That chills the heart with sadness ruefully.

The nightingale whose stirring notes arise,
    And swell aloft the dom'ed heaven to touch,
Swift to the heart the feeling cadence flies
    And leaves a gloom, yet we desire it much.

To tread soft paths with lively flowers fringed;
    To music hear that quickening pulses roam;
Enlivened all, and naught the gildings singed,
    Is not enough to give the heart a home.

Fate did his work, but only after death,
    That monster dread had wrought his cruel task;
They praise no more for want of vital breath,
    And ask it not for want of it to ask.

The Muse's song is not a lay of mirth,
    But love is there and spices every turn.
These modest lines may not the gist unearth,
    But buried still in antiquated urn.

When all is still and Nature sinks to rest;
   A pleasant gloom o'erspreads the neighboring hills;
A burning sun has sunk within the west;
   No sound is heard save laughing of the rills;

And when the stillness weaves, within the heart,
   A woof of pain the few past years have seen;
When pierced by some unknown, unwarning dart,
   And all the sorrow from the past will glean;

Then hear my lay, though my poor pen portray,
   In feeble lines, the picture as it should.
If God but bless His old time gracious way
   As th' lovely saint for doing what she could.

I.

Some six decades have passed since she was here,
   And winds wail o'er her undiscovered tomb,
A requiem sad that e'en the wolf would fear,
   And chill a heart possessed of common gloom.

The ocean waves roll o'er the grave of her,
   Who fathoms deep with brilliant coral lays,
Imbedded where the ocean workmen stir,
   Which once was beauty in her living days.

So at her grave there reads no passer by
   That here lies what was beauty, once, and love,
That decked a household with its brilliant eye,
   That had a heart as great as woman's prove.

That loved her hours of pleasure just as we,
   That often smiled and gladdened other hearts,
That loved the romance of the trysting tree
   And led men captive with her gentle arts.

That wept when sorrow drew his curtains o'er,
   And beauty still shone through the falling tear,
And tho't of heav'n where she should weep no more
   And bid farewell to all things transient here.

Tho' marble tells not of her living here,
   Nor e'en the day God bade her soul depart
From flesh and blood into a spirit's sphere,
   'Tis written still in tablets of the heart.

II.

In early days her noted father, kind,
   Had taught her much and urged her to her task;
Instruction sent that she might store her mind,
   To know the truth and ne'er its teachings mask.

She learned the arts and scanned the classic page,
   The poet's song was to her blissful hours,
The masters read that live from age to age
   Within these hearts and energize the powers.

On Richmond Hill her happy days were spent,
   When youth and beauty graced her fairy form.
To graceful culture all her powers were lent,
   But never dreamed to meet the days of storm.

And in those days she learned her father's worth,
   His stately step, his captivating eye,
His honored rank in nation best of earth
   Had called her love to pass his errings by.

When love once knit within a woman's breast,
   Is firm unmoved no matter what the wrong,
She loves him still as one among the blest,
   As friends forsake, grows many times more strong.

So when at last the Myrmidon chief
  Had prostrate fallen by one imprudent blow,
She loves him still, and, saddened with his grief,
  Praised for his deeds as ladies only do.

III.

At early age their happy threshold crossed
  A suitor from the bright and sunny south.
His mission fair his feeling heart engrossed,
  Which stole fair words from out his stammering
    mouth.

Often he came and sought the lady's side,
  And oft she sighed to know the reason why;
Forever pressed with true and wonted pride,
  No lady loves 'twould pass this question by.

Until one eve when up the sloping hill
  He came again with quick and stately tread,
Her sparkling eyes with visions of him fill,
  She quickly thinks of words that he has said.

Of words, indeed, that might be words of truth,
  But much is false, so she had need beware;
She found no fault, not once was he uncouth,
  And dreamed of when his every joy should share.

But now he comes, they talk of current things,
  When o'er with this he turns to solemner thought;
He plights his love, this one request he brings,
  More than the world her heart and hand he sought.

Then waits reply; she blushing bows her head,
  Sits silent long and weighs the question o'er.
He urges suit in words profoundly said,
  From poets' gleans and men of ancient lore.

She answers not, from time to time he waits,
   She fairer seems for making this a task.
'Tis sweet to wait, the drawn suspense well freights
   The heart with that which makes it joy to ask.

Until at last the blest assent is given
   That wafts suspense and a gladder "seem" possessed
Of agent fair, the principle of heaven,
   With all the former doubts and fears redressed.

IV.

The wedding o'er, they sped their wandering way
   O'er hill and vale, o'er wood and plain alone.
It grieved her sore that she should part to-day
   From him who gave in early years a home.

But this the fate of those who learn to love;
   Their early ties must sever with the years,
Assuming care and striving as they strove
   Whom now they leave with heart pangs and with
      tears.

Now days pass by and wearily on they go
   Thro' Jersey soil and Maryland as well,
Virginia's clime, where crystal waters flow,
   They leave behind, as many a story tell.

Not spiritless, though there are pangs of woe,
   None would return, though have some regret,
But such is life, and those who onward go
   Make sacrifice for all the joys they get.

Far in the south the weary wanderers rest,
   And take abode in pleasant mansions there,
By a sunny stream of Carolina blest,
   Whose lovely soil saw maiden ne'er so fair.

V.

For many years in pleasant circles there
 She lived and moved for other happier hearts,
And felt the weight of that paternal care
 And blessed it much with all her treasured arts.

She often wrote and told him of her care,
 Assured him much she was her father's child.
In lonely hours she cheered his musings there
 When public life had wrought ambition wild.

The little son which Theodosia loved,
 When he had fallen, her father hoped to see
Regain his fame, perpetuate unmoved
 His high-born name in manly purity.

He pictured courts, his grandchild as the chief,
 And manly forms obeisance to him do.
And land and wealth with not a cloud of grief,
 A million subjects to him ever true.

But for her sire fair Theodosia sighed,
 His presence calm was always heaven to her,
The public mind, for him, her praise defied.
 To forgive divine and human 'tis to err.

From Briton's isle and Holland's sunken coast,
 From fairy France his words of cheering came,
And she admires—a fallen man at most,
 Almost adores his much derided name.

Outcast from home, abroad, mistrusted still,
 Reduced to want and poverty and shame,
Wandering far, with hope his fancies fill,
 His errings were far better than a name.

In all his woe he had a joy for her,
 In all his want a wealth 'twas ne'er surpassed,
In wanderings far a home his yearnings were.
 Love's tie ne'er breaks for leagues nor hatred's blast.

VI.

But now, alas! another heavy cloud,
 Dark as the night threatening to rave,
Her smiling boy was wrapped within the shroud,
 And, cold in death, was laid down in the grave.

Blessed childhood, when pearly teardrops fall,
 And leave no trace of anguish on the cheek.
To be a child when present is the all,
 The Master said was semblance of the meek.

There's none but loves the prattle of a child,
 Its innocence knits many a lasting tie.
A mother's love is e'en a passion wild,
 'Twould suffer death than see her darling die.

She saw him once when in his chamber there
 He lay asleep and dreamed at pleasant dreams.
And then she smiled and tho't his waking fair,
 But now she weeps nor hopes for better means.

At death friends weep, and hope drives off the tears,
 But not so now, for days have intervened.
But still she grieves and friends expressing fears,
 No other thought her heart of love can wean.

VII.

From Europe's soil he strives to sail away,
 For weeks and months in anxious readiness.
A native land, tho' least the welcome may
 Enchant him there, surpasses homelessness.

For he who strays from clime to clime afar,
    Moves restless on, for wonders still the cry,
Will seek the land wherein his boy-days were,
    Ere life is closed and lay down there to die.

And so to port at last the wanderer came,
    To spend the evening of his life at home.
This man that once was honored with a name,
    Which now dishonored, leaves him narrow, lone.

VIII.

Her father came, she hears this news with hope
    That he will banish all her clouds apace,
And hastens hence with dreadful wave to cope,
    She heeds them not to see her father's face.

The year was old, and Time had turned his beard
    From livid hue to cold and waning gray.
This lovely plant was as all Nature seared,
    And needs a fount 'twould wash this death away.

'Tis sad to know of such a heart as this,
    That lives to love when blasted every care.
'Tis sad to feel she knew no other bliss
    Than transientness within this mundane sphere.

Tho' she might hope to meet her boy again,
    And clasp him in a brighter world than this;
Then she should joy to know him free from pain,
    Endearment more than of a mother's kiss.

The morn has come, she is to bid adieu
    To kindred friends and trust the billowy sea;
For there as well 'neath God's protection too,
    No dangers hold, this side mortality.

With solemn mein fair Theodosia still
   Unaltered sits and ne'er dispelled by hope.
Tho' fancy gleams, that void can never fill,
   It pains to act, so gives her sorrow scope.

Last night she dreamed that on a gentle hill
   Her darling boy and she were gathering flowers,
Which gaily shone reflecting beauty still,
   And seemed to gladden all the fleeting hours.

Ne'er vain to dream since God has granted power,
   If not abused by turning to the wrong.
It gives a joy altho' deceptive hour,
   And calms the spirit that it may be strong.

They talked of him and tho't he soon would come,
   Whom they had loved and wished for e'er so long
To give him rest within their pleasant home;
   The old man cheer who ever suffered wrong.

They seemed as children there to sit and watch,
   And quaintly talked, as little children do.
The zephyrs play the pleasant foliage stretch,
   As if looking earnest for a loved one, too.

As dreams when sad, at waking give a joy,
   While sad we seem because of moments past,
So dreams when glad repress with this alloy,
   And glad we seem because of guild o'ercast.

She tho't they saw him coming o'er the hills;
   Their hearts beat glad, their bright eyes sparkling
      gleam,
And then she wakes and starts with gladness still
   And learns it was a fair, delusive dream.

IX.

The ship was strong, and *Patriot* was her name,
  Well worth the care of daughters of the land;
And one so fair would brighten its fair fame
  If spared by storm and rock and reef and sand.

The clouds were gray, the sea was blurred with haze,
  The sun was hid—it seemed a task to shine
To cheer the ones who never more should gaze
  In friendly glance on those she left behind.

But on she went, the *Patriot* sailed from port,
  The gentle breeze bid fair to drive them thro';
Their songs were sung, enlivening was their sport
  Which whiled the hours from many unto few.

The cheery voice was heard of those on deck,
  The sun shone o'er the wide extended sea,
The dim-marked shore, for which they little reck,
  Far in the west the merry crowd may see.

The eve was calm before the awful day.
  The night swept on, no token gave of ill,
And fancy flew in dreams—he had full sway
  And pictured fair of bygone pleasures still.

In early morn they saw a stranger bark
  And waited for a time to know its name.
Oh, heed not now, for it is death to hark,
  But strive as deer to flee the hunter's game.

But ah! too late! The wily craft o'ercame,
  Suppressed the crew to dire obeisance there.
Their pleading cursed, their prayers all in vain,
  Announced their fate, the strong as well as fair.

But 'tis not Briton's sons who cruelly
   Bring such destruction on th' unhappy crew,
'Tis pirates, scourging far the briny sea
   And granting life as wickedness will do.

They howl destruction as a wolf so rude,
   Their victims all command to walk the plank.
Their eyeballs glare as on their course pursued,
   Those forty victims, who 'neath the billows sank.

The time of Theodosia came at last.
   She plead of him, who gave the stern command,
To grant this one as time to her most past,
   Some time with God for guidance by His hand.

Some time to plead and make her peace with Him,
   And grant her grace beyond this vale of tears;
Some time to ask a pardon for her sin,
   And that His love would cast out all her fear.

"Go," said the chief, "and make it very short."
   She went.   Not long she came again in white
As if a bride, she seemed to smile in sport
   With faith in Him who doeth all things right.

Up to her breast she held the blessed book
   That teaches men the way of truth and life;
She wept a tear and gave to heaven a look,
   And those stern hearts with feelings deep were rife.

The leader sighed, "Ah, me, that I were true,
   But gone too long these rugged ways of mine,
There's no retreat but kill, tho' I must rue
   This beastly sin; for angels ne'er outshine.

The pirate paused, that had the task to do,
   And would have spared, but others said him no.

At stern command she walked the dread plank, too,
  And sank a victim to the waves below.

Her whitened bones now lay beneath the wave,
  For many years the billows o'er her roll;
Unsought, unknown, lies in a watery grave,
  May Heaven grant peace and joy unto her soul.

⁂

The Church of Eberdown.

WITHIN a valley far away from sea or inland
  town—
Just where a little streamlet poured its sparkling wa-
  ters down,
And, growing larger as it flowed on with gentle rill,
And stronger, when its current grew it turned the old
  gray mill.
The rough hewed mountains on the east were high
  and grand, sublime,
And verdant as the valley till they reach the snowy
  clime;
And oft their hoary heads of snow, just when the day
  was done,
Seemed sending back like precious gems the gladness
  of the sun.
Just at its base, 'neath evergreens, 'tis in my memory
  still,
As verdant as those trees e'er were which that enclos-
  ure fill—
The dearest, purest place on earth in country or in
  town,

And that's the blessed little church—the church of
    Eberdown.

And oft we laughed on Sabbath morn, for we were
    children then,
When solemn rang the old church bell to call us chil-
    dren in.
Tho' from our family 'twere but two, my sister Sue
    and I,
Yet from my father's cot there came a larger family.
For the village children gathered there, and from our
    cot we'd go,
All laughing, to that dear old church where the hon-
    eysuckles grow.
We passed within the vestibule, and up the old church
    aisle,
All smiling were our faces, and our hearts were free
    from guile,
And when the parson prayed a prayer we bowed our
    youthful heads,
And our little hearts went up to Him who little chil-
    dren leads;
And when he gave a hymn to sing, of heaven or of
    home,
The sweetest lay we sang, 'twas then, in the church of
    Eberdown.

And when the parson preached, we sat, and to his
    word give heed;
He told us of the one who loved and gave us every
    need;
And after he had finished quite, had sung and prayed
    again,

'Twas then the benediction came to children and to
　　men,
For all the little town was there, the old as well as
　　young—
The old had lost their smiling face, had lost their
　　ready tongue;
So we were left alone in glee, my little mates and I,
To think of naught but merriment, to bid all sorrow
　　fly.
And when the parson said, "Amen," we quietly and
　　slow
Went out upon the green again within the sun's bright
　　glow.
For many a spot was beautiful within that little town,
But none were half so beautiful as the church of Eber-
　　down.

Just to the south a little way our ready feet oft went,
Where stood the neatly carved stone and lofty monu-
　　ment.
And oft when we had said our prayers and sung our
　　little hymn,
We'd go from out the old church door upon the
　　churchyard green,
We'd read upon the marble slab of those then gone
　　before,
And think that they await us upon the other shore.
But not a sorrow made us sigh and not a tear we gave;
We played upon the little mound that marked a lone-
　　ly grave.
And when the evening sun had set—its farewell glance
　　had given,
We'd wend our ways toward our homes, and leave the
　　rest to heaven;

And at our mother's knee at home we, gently kneeling
    down,
Would pray to heaven as at the church—the church of
    Eberdown.

Now, when the early Autumn came, the leaves began
    to fade,
The grass began to grow so brown in sunshine or in
    shade.
Just as their verdure went away and faded out of
    sight,
My sister Sue did fade away upon a solemn night.
This sorrow was my first, so deep, and oh! it grieved
    my heart
To know together we had played and now for aye
    must part.
But little sister, as she died, looked up and smiled to
    me,
And said, around the great white throne bright angels
    she could see;
And then she asked if I would go and list to angel's
    song.
And be with her on heaven's green among the white
    robed throng.
But, while the tears flowed down my cheeks, that
    prayer I could not own,
For God had willed that I should stay at the church
    of Eberdown.

So when the morn had come again, the sun shone
    bright and fair,
They opened up a casket white and placed my sister
    there.

The parson came and sang a hymn, and prayed and
    sang again,
Then to the church they took her form—'twas born by
    stalwart men,
And up that aisle she went again, as oft she had of
    yore;
But 'twas a sorrow deep to know that she should go
    no more.
The parson read the Master's word of bidding chil-
    dren come,
And said that she was surely blessed within her heav-
    enly home;
But then it grieved me more than all that she should
    happy be,
And I should never see her face, save in eternity;
Still all the grief, tho' solemn full, a shade 'twas of
    God's frown
Had knit within a stronger cord for the church of
    Eberdown.

They bore her little form again out through the open
    door,
We knew that form we loved so well should pass that
    way no more.
The quiet shade of th' dear old trees put on a solemn
    air,
And the smiling flowers now drooped their heads, and
    all seemed weeping there;
And thro' the churchyard gate we went, my parents
    dear and I,
And passed unto that awful grave where little Sue
    must lie.
And O! what sorrow 'twas to me when the doleful
    clods did fall,

They gave a tear-drop to each eye and cast a gloom
  o'er all.
So then we left her there alone in sunshine or in rain;
And oft when even' shadows came I sought for her
  again;
But all that's left of her to cheer is the little verdant
  mound
Within the churchyard near the church—the church of
  Eberdown.

And when the autumn days were gone, my father went
  away,
We placed him in the churchyard, too, upon a winter
  day.
And mother, too, was called away to follow father
  home,
The angels bore her spirit blest up thro' the azure
  dome;
And I can fancy now that she and little Sue look down
And smile a smile for aye to me behind a seeming
  frown.
So I was left an orphan lone with none to care for me,
For somehow christians pray for us with little charity;
And to a stranger's mind we're bad, 'tis always plain
  and fair,
If we were true as we should be we'd find a shelter
  there;
And so there's scarce a charity for the orphans of the
  town,
And I was left with the little church—the church of
  Eberdown.

Thro' many kicks and many cuffs, and many sighs
  and tears,

I grew to be almost a man, and full a man in years.
Still one there was who smiled on me—she pretty was
    and good.
I thought I saw a gleam of light while I in darkness
    stood.
So to the old church once again, remembered of them
    all,
'Twas not to follow prostrate dead, 'twas not to bear
    the pall,
For 'twas a merry party went the day that I was wed;
The parson called us "man and wife"—'twas her I
    gently led.
So down the old church aisle again I went with cheeks
    aglow;
My heart was swelling full with joy this happiness to
    know.
For four short months of happiness, without a tear or
    frown,
We lived within a little cot near the church of Eber-
    down.

But then one morn in autumn sere, just as my sister
    Sue,
The angel came and took my own to be an angel, too.
So in the churchyard she was laid, the one so young
    and fair,
And oft I wished that I might be an inmate with her
    there.
Oft when the Sabbath sermon's done I'd to the church-
    yard go,
And, weeping o'er four lonely mounds that lay there
    in a row,
Would say a prayer, all solemn 'twas by the sorrow
    God had given,

That I might pass the road they'd gone, and be with
　　them in heaven;
For earth is all a dreary land when we are left alone,
'Tis better far to be at rest and dwell with God at
　　home.
But still there's aught on earth for me within this lit-
　　tle town,
And that's the blessed little church—the church of
　　Eberdown.

But I've trudged on for many years since they have
　　gone away,
Till now my eyes are dim with tears, my locks are
　　turning gray;
And not far hence I know I'll see the angel coming
　　down
To bear my weary spirit far up to that glorious home.
I've learned one thing in passing thro', which every
　　person might,
That which we love as beautiful oft passes from our
　　sight,
And then there's sadness in our hearts, that dream of
　　joy is o'er,
For beauties are just out of reach upon this transient
　　shore.
The angel comes and holds aloft, lifts high a warning
　　hand
And bids us wait until we reach that fairer, better land.
And so I'm waiting now to go and reap what I have
　　sown,
And pass, as long ago they passed, through the church
　　of Eberdown.

Rosalie.

I OFT have heard the harp in sadness sing
  And watched the nimble fingers strike each chord;
The solemn cadence of each note would bring
  A meaning, like the cadence of a word.

I oft have heard the tales of lovers told
  And watched the bright tear sparkle on the cheek,
And every word as banes to me unfold,
  Deep in my heart a dread asylum seek.

I oft have gazed upon the western sky
  And saw the glorious "King of Day" depart.
The evening birds across my path would fly,
  And unseen spirits sadly grieve my heart.

I oft have sought the busy cares of life
  To drown the pangs my earlier years have known;
Of sadness calm, or pain in sadder strife,
  Adown the path, each object me has shown.

I oft have tho't my pangs of heart were full
  And wondered so that others more should grieve;
"'Twas weakness that their sadness would not lull,
  Affected weakness that would go at leave."

So thus I sat beneath the boughs of youth
  And gathered fruit from off forbidden trees,
And driven .from the fields of right and truth,
  The flaming sword forbids me all that ease.

We never know the pain that others feel,
  Tho' sympathize we with them e'er so much;

Their keenest sorrows to us ne'er reveal
   Until, our hearts, those keenest sorrows touch.

Some word untold or told at evil hours,
   Because a selfish heart would wish it else,
Will give a bane beyond all human powers.
   All joy is gone.   The heart with sorrow melts.

The harvest time has come for me at last;
   The turtledove is cooing on the eave.
Its mournful story brings to me the past,
   And gives a sadness that will never leave.

I saw a flower; no fairer earth e'er had,
   And often worshiped at that idol shrine.
That beauteous grace could never make me sad,
   Could kill no joy within this heart of mine.

The mystic sun from out the mystic skies
   Would shed a glory o'er its petals sweet,
Tho' shadows came, that grace rose to my eyes,
   And shed its fragrance at my very feet.

But why will mortals stoop to mortal forms
   And worship as if God upon the throne?
No shelter will they give in direst storm,
   And, needing help, we're left to sigh alone.

That flower a maiden fair has walked the earth,
   Has smiled like angels smile on saintly forms,
And hers the purest laugh well fraught with mirth,
   The brightest eyes that mortal e'er adorn.

Her eyelids closed o'er half that beauteous mold
   That gave a luster of the brightest gray;
Her lashes oft a gentle tear would hold;
   Her looks would truly melt a heart away.

She sang the purest, sweetest earthly lays,
   The nightingale would sneak away outvied;
The cuckoo with his loudest notes would praise,
   And oft 'twould cheer her at the brooklet side.

Oft when the evening sun was sinking low,
   The robin sought his eve-accustomed place.
The piercing notes which him enraptured so,
   Were sung full long with such a vaunting grace.

The maiden sat upon the porch below,
   And smiled to hear him sing with wildest glee,
And graceful as the swift and gentle roe,
   But far below the song of Rosalie.

One simple trill the robin blushed with shame,
   But that upon his face was hard to see.
He hid his head beneath his downy wing
   And would not hear the song of Rosalie.

How oft adown the old and winding path
   We wandered at the closing of the day,
And plucked the rose to make the flowery wreath,
   And crown the brooklet on its shining way.

Upon a stone beside an olden cot
   We sat and watched the little brooklet go.
Those youthful days can never be forgot;
   They will return and ridicule our woe.

The stone was mossy and the cot was low,
   Just at our feet there grew the ivy vine;
And o'er our heads, the cot was rotting slow,
   There hung the red-hued blooming eglantine.

How oft she sang those sweetest songs of hers,
   That came like notes from far off Paradise,

I tho't me blest like good old Jacob was,
   And saw a heaven in those sparkling eyes.

One Autumn eve ere yet the frost had seared
   The trees and meadow with its fatal breath;
Or chilly winter with his snowy beard
   Had bound the flowers unto icy death;

The same old path adown we went again
   With jest and laugh of youthful perfect glee,
No cares of rich nor tho't of prudent men
   Could I ere have with bonny Rosalie.

When rising high I heard the skylark sing,
   The robin chirped within the verdant trees,
The nightingale sang just below the spring,
   His piercing notes made rife the evening breeze.

The harsh voiced snipe upon the mead did call,
   And, rising high, went whistling up afar,
Assayed to scale the top of Heaven's wall,
   But lost his strength upon the silent air.

The housedog barked along the winding way,
   Adown the same I came with Rosalie.
All nature stirred beneath the golden gray,
   All nature sang to fill our hearts with glee.

One single note, the lady by my side
   Pealed forth upon the air, so full of glee,
And every sound that felt its presence hied,
   They could not stay the notes of Rosalie.

One little song and everything was hushed,
   All nature strained to silence in the hour,
Her youthful face with radiant beauty gushed,
   And simply smiled that I should know her power.

The sweetest hour God ever gave to man
   Was in the dream of love in early days;
When bright eyed youth and maiden seek to ban,
   Ecstatic, tho'tless as a bird of praise.

But up the path I went with Rosalie—
   I little dreamed that this would be the last,
But heaven was kind to will it thus to me,
   No sorrow cloud this hour would then o'ercast.

Her voice was tranquil and her heart was glad,
   A sweet "good-night" she said, as oft before,
When sunset parting at the brooklet side,
   Or later parting at the cottage door.

We trod the loved old path adown no more,
   Or gazed upon the golden sun at eve,
Thro' time agone I catch a gleam of yore,
   And hear the lispings that the angels breathe.

I seem so near the Paradise of Peace,
   I catch the fragrance of the flowers there,
And see the glory that will never cease
   Within the portals of that Aiden fair.

Where'er the feet of Rosalie are gone,
   The smiling muse insists I shall not say.
What know I, save that I am left alone,
   Without the song and laugh of Rosalie?

'Twas early morn when last I saw her face;
   Upon the slope I bade the sad adieu,
And breathed a prayer that God would give her grace,
   And breathed a prayer that I might e'er be true.

Tho' she may live upon this earth of ours—
   May live and laugh and still be full of glee;

And give to friends her simple, childlike powers.
Yet, certain 'tis, that she is dead to me.

ىئە

Time and Eternity.

THE weakness of my mortal frame, I own,
Revolts to limit in the things I know.
The talents given at my Maker's hand
Can make me only hope and trust and pray
For Heaven's help in such attempt as this.
And that the muse of Greek mythology
May be an entity of purest truth,
The product of the mighty and of heaven.
That muse that bends its heart to valiant deeds
Of war, the enemy of brotherhood,
Or turns unto the selfish love of man,
Is not the muse to lift our souls heavenward,
But, chained to dote on forms of nothingness,
And never live to any higher end.

When God, the architect of their frail ship,
Had launched it from the port Eternity,
And bid it sail and then return again
Unto the port of starting, sure, he meant
To have it sail for purpose grand.
                   So may I dwell
Upon the somber, solemn ways of earth
And melody of Heaven. So may I
A picture draw of vivid scenes of time,
E'en down to borders of Infinity;
And, resting there, may turn my mortal eyes

Far up the azure walls of Heaven's dome
And say, Thy word is sure, I trust Thee, Lord.

But calm and gentle muse, now give me strength
To follow forth a wondering, loving twain,
Whose hearts a beating in full harmony
Their plighted love will greatly modify
Their destiny, than if they walked alone
The path of life, e'en for their good.
                              And then
The twain adown the thorny path of life
Had started hand in hand that very day,
The fitting earthly-lasting knot was tied,
That grates not on the honest human soul,
But rather lifts it up to bear the pangs
Of life.   Each to the other tells their grief
And sheds the crystal tear together.
And each the other tells their little joys,
And laugh together as they tell it;
And looking to the other's sunny face
Of seeming psychal sunshine beaming rays,
Their joy swells forth, and like the rose of spring
That grows along a gravelly, thorny path,
That when footsore full half its terrors go
At sight of these; so goes our earthly life.
The wily snares of Satan speak to them
In muffled whispers, 'tis a grave revolt,
So speak they low, Jehovah's ministers,
And bid them think upon the course they take,
That lest it, seeming right, may lead astray
And be the bane that crushes in the end.

So on they go and often dream a dream
Of happiness beyond this mortal sphere.

Sometimes they loiter in their useful journey,
Forget the object of their toil in going,
And so defer their journey hitherward.
They credit not what is not understood,
And suits their evil inclinations not,
Yet truth, and God its truthful author,
And older than error much, much older,
Lasting for ever and ever and ever.
As God has ways that are higher than ours,
So we, like little children, think we go
Upon a hobby-horse a journey far
And learning much when we are standing still
And dreaming.   But they, like St. Peter,
When in the hour of over confidence
In self insinuating devils lead
Astray and they deny their chosen lord,
The warning cock his holy mission fills
And they, to penance given, weep bitterly.

So ever and anon the path seems rough,
And they, grown weary as they travel on,
Accuse the morn that gave them starting,
And wish the end would come and give them
     rest—
That rest, so sweet, to those who grown aweary.

Twas on a calm, bright eve of summer time.
The golden sun aslant the deep-hued west
Cast forth his rings of undulating luster,
And as he neared the horizontal plane
His seeming farewells cast a hopeful look
As if to say, "We'll meet again."   But no;
There's one that ne'er shall look upon thy face,
Unless thy ways are seen by spirit eyes,
And thou givest light to those in other worlds.

I saw them walking down the path of life
And come unto the dreaded river, Death;
Their locks had lost no useful luster yet,
Their faces bright, no wrinkles on their brow,
And all 'twas seen, was little tints of care
To note their marching on.   The mother goes,
The wife of him, her mate who helped to weave
His fortune, or mend his woe.

They gather at the river brink and wait
For that they long so not to see, and still
'Tis only short the distance to that other world
Of rest beyond.   Upon the sandy shore
Of the vast and billowy rolling sea,
There sometimes friendly faces meet to part.
Across the raging, foaming ocean some go,
And some are left behind.   They say farewell.
It may be for all time, but hoping still
To meet upon this transient shore again.
It may be for eternity, that tho't
Is lost in brighter hopes, and so they bring
A solace to themselves and shed the tear
Of parting.   Hard at the river death they part,
They meet on shore of time no more, indeed,
Nor, maybe, in eternity.

                        Now she they loved.
Assayed to pass the stream, but lingered still,
And wished to journey longer in the world,
And be with those she loved, but she must go.
Her husband and her children gather round
To bid the last, the sad adieu we feel
So much.   And she alone assured a calm,
And bade them weep not tho' she longed to stay;
That they'd come soon and meet her there,

And be together with the blest for aye.
"I'm going home, but oh! the way is dark,
No glimmer of the bright beyond
My waning earthly eyes can see, but wait
I till the journey's done.
        "Dear ones, meet me
In the brighter, better fields of Eden,
Where we shall know no earthly woe."
And then they took her by the hand to bid
The last adieu.
        Two boys approaching,
Who wept as if their youthful hearts would break;
They could not say farewell, but wished it much.
And then a little girl with soft black eyes
And curly, silken, raven locks that hung
In pretty tresses o'er her neck, and said,
"Good bye," and asked if she would come again
And tell the good of mansions fair above,
The Master long ago had gone to build;
Or whether when she reached the golden gate—
The portals of that far off glory land—
She would not ask the good old saint to let
Her little girl, a pretty maid of earth,
Go thro' the portals fair of Heaven's gate.

She passed away. They could not farther go,
But wept aloud when she was passing o'er.
The children soon forgot their sorrow sore,
The husband learned to bear it without tears,
And hoped and prayed that they might meet again.
But, turn we to the one that's gone before,
Oblivion held her thro' the chilling tide.
She woke to find herself in Paradise,
She heard the music of that heavenly sphere,

She heard the welcome of the angels near;
The song they sang she had not heard before,
Which mortals dare not sing on earthly shores.
She saw the throne on which the I Am sits,
Much whiter than the driven snow below;
She saw the glory of the Father there,
And o'er His head hung shining, golden clouds
In which angels bathed their silver wings.
Attendant angels for His bidding wait,
And sing his glory thro' the efflorescent air;
The crystal sea, its beauteous waters flow
In ripples to the music of the harp.
Along the shores quintescent with the rays
Of light celestial, are seen and heard
The angel throng with robes as white as snow.
A chorus strong they sing, which makes the heart
To swell tumultuous, and in its growth
Learn more to love the kindred angel beings.

When these she saw and heard, then she forgot
The beings of that mundane lower world,
Her soul absorbed within the light celestial.
There is no weeping and no sorrow there;
In all the endless realm of that country
Is felt the fullness of tangible love.
We only know it here as quality,
But there a veritably pure essence,
Unlimited, illimitable.

And these the lofty words of welcome grand,
She heard them greet her with, "Come, blest one,
Receive the glory God will give to thee,
Prepared in myriads of years agone,
And reign with us thro' all eternity."
Thank God, no shade of envy enters Heaven,

But with each other holy angels live,
And to each other all the honors give.
With these environments we closely gaze,
To see her turn unto her former days,
But she turns not. We list to hear her sigh
In yearning for the ones on mortal shores,
But she sighs not. Her soul absorbed
By grander ties than e'er conceived beneath
The skies. She thinks no more of earth nor hell—
Their mournful imperfections dwell alone
In lower spheres. And tho' I delve beneath
The briny sea a hundred fathoms deep,
And soar aloft beyond the topmost clouds,
Go east and west and north and south alike
In distance far, and gather all the gems
In one quintescent heap, I ne'er can give
The feeblest picture of the glory there.
She donned the robe in which the angels fly,
She caught the glitterings that the spirit gives,
In ecstacy she softly soared aloft,
And smiled a smile that mortals never know,
And as she rose to greet the great I Am
The myriad choir of Heaven shouted loud
One long and glorious "hallelujah."
It was so grand that I can ne'er describe,
It was so good that I can ne'er portray,
It was so large that angels never mete
Tho' measure they thro' all eternity,

The Parting.

WHEN hopes arise they often die
    And live no more forever,
As sadly past the moments fly
    The earnest ties will sever.
The ways of Heaven are not our ways,
Tho' sad, the player sings his lays,
    "Forever and forever."

    The sun may rise and smiling seem
        Upon the sparkling river;
    The birds may flit, their rays may gleam
        With an ecstatic quiver.
But curtains come across the skies,
And hopes will fail and fear arise
        Forever and forever.

    Down at the garden gate they stand,
        The matron and the maiden.
    A youth has won the maiden's hand,
        She goes with blessings laden;
They gave a parting glance of love,
A bird sang from a twig above,
        "Forever and forever."

    A youth upon the threshold stands,
        The parting blessing given;
    The birthright lay within his hands,
        He trusts the rest to heaven.
But on that threshold, loved of yore,

The laughing boy will go no more
    Forever and forever.

A man may tread the way of life
    With kindred spirits near him,
With truest love or trifling strife
    And many a one to cheer him.
But, as the breezes near him glide,
He glides and leaves his youth and pride
    Forever and forever.

The rays, that fall from yonder sun
    And dart across the river,
Have silvered o'er the old man's head
    And stole its youthful luster.
Tho' Heaven's hopes are fully bright,
The old man's years have taken flight
    Forever and forever.

So thus he sits with palsied hand
    And looks beyond the river,
And waits to hear Death's dole command
    And feel the cold darts shiver;
And then, glance back, unto the way
His feet shall walk no more for aye—
    Forever and forever.

Jeremiah Jenkins' Mistake.

THOSE who love a pretty story,
  Solemn, comic, sad or gory,
    False or true, it matters not,
If the soul's enrapt with wonder,
As 'twere the distant rumbling thunder,
    That they quite forget the plot
        To entrance them,
And they at the author's will
        To enhance them,
In the heart a yearning pleasure fills.

As they love to laugh or pity
In the sonnet or the ditty,
    So they love to share the good
When they hear a story golden,
Hap'ning late, or romance olden,
    It will give the soul no food,
        Till 'tis told them,
And some join with smile or tears
        As 'tis told them,
And raise within them anxious, longing fears.

Now within a little village,
Free from miser's pomp or pillage,
    On a western sloping hill.
Oft in summer evening olden
Set the sun in west so golden
    That many merry hearts would fill
        With grandeur keenly;

And such a silence there would dwell,
  A calm serenely,
Which only felt, no mortal e'er can tell.

Oft the sunburnt urchin shouted,
And the peasant gaily routed
 In the midst of romp and cheer;
Oft the old folks sat in summer,
And their stories without number,
  Mystic, wierd that chilled with fear
   Told so ghostly;
Yet they gave a secret pleasure
   While relating,
And the impress last without erasure.

Many a Sabbath morning came,
Hallowed with a blessed name,
 And a golden sparkling sun;
Many a youth and maid were seen,
'Neath the foliage of green,
 Coursing to the church beyond.
   And the cheer,
 As if from the world above,
   Heavenly sphere,
Where there's naught but peace and joy and love.

In the church their voices rise,
With the angels of the skies,
 His glorious praises sing;
And bowing there devoutly pray
For guidance in the better way;
 And by His grace to safely bring
   Their talents home,
 And have them doubled for his care

In blessing them,
And be the ones received in mansions fair.

But, to my tale.   Within the town
There stood a little cottage brown,
   Hid from view by verdant trees;
The inmates of the cottage there,
A widow and her daughter fair,
   Composed a lonely family,
         But happy still.
   And oft the cooling evening breeze
         With song would fill,
From out the cottage 'neath the waving trees.

The maid was young and gay and fair,
And to a fortune she was heir,
   Yet she was never vain;
The poorest she would welcome in,
Relieve distress and chide the sin
   Of those who were to blame,
         In such a way
   That they could not deride;
         And they would pray
For such a joy as hers and then be satisfied

Her widowed mother to her kind,
Had a tender heart and sterner mind,
   By prudence she was guided;
And always sought to teach her child
To give the erring each a smile,
   But e'er her trust confided
         To her mother;
   And they oft asked in prayer,
         From another,
For His presence with them ever and His care.

On a farm some miles away,
Stood a mansion many a day,
  Of a thrifty countryman,
Who plowed his ground and sowed his seed,
And never stood an hour in need
  Of food or clothes from any hand,
      Save from above;
  And so he cleared and tilled his farm.
      Who willing prove,
May learn a lesson that will keep from harm.

He had a son, a stalwart boy,
Who was a constant source of joy,
  In his first and twentieth year.
His plans so practically wise,
He thought his son would surely rise,
  In thot's and riches every year,
      "Till some would know"—
This said the old man with a smile,
      "A Jenkins, too,
'Twill take no bride his spirits to defile."

So like young men, this young man too,
Thought some kind maiden's heart to woo,
  In the very latest way.
He donned his best attire one morn,
Ane left his father at the corn,
  And in his carriage sped away.
      "Gone a courting,"
  Was the verdict of the father,
      Wife retorting,
"Jeremiah Jenkins, did he really?"

Rumors steadily came round,
'Twas the gossip of the town,

Isabella had a beau;
And they twitted Isabel,
She would smile and blush as well,
    Till they really thought 'twas so,
            And 'twas so;
    For in all the country round,
            Whispers low,
Where the sober, gallant, robust man was found.

Oft when stopped he at the gate,
When the day was growing late,
    He could hear the lady's voice,
Singing as the cuckoo sings,
As she sits above the springs;
    And it makes his heart rejoice.
            But the discord
    Of another's harshly swell,
            Formed the discord.
"Jeremiah Jenkens, Isabel."

Jeremiah, practical,
Thinks his suit succeeding well,
    He will gain the maiden;
But to risk no devastation,
He will make investigation,
    Far more the cash will gladden.
            So one morning,
    He goes to make his bargain sure;
            Brilliant morning,
Could his love such tricks as this endure?

To the court house off he goes,
Never gives a thought of woes,
    For the error of to-day;
Seeks the records of the land,

And then of the cash in hand;
The bargain certainly will pay,
With the maiden;
Then returns he to his home
Mental laden,
Mostly with the hope of monetary gain.

Jeremiah Jenkins, halt,
Friends have seen thy grievous fault,
Will inform another;
Such an imposition none
Will suffer to that fairest one—
The fact was told the mother,
And then straight
A note the facts did tell.
"Now, don't wait
On Jeremiah Jenkins, Isabel."

Jeremiah never comes,
And her mind full often roams
To days now long gone by;
And watches, sometimes hoping still
That he her wishes will fulfil;
And never knew his reason why,
For thus staying
And break a gay and modest heart,
Still she's praying
For antidote from this poison dart.

Jeremiah his error knew,
And told it to but very few;
But still, practically
Never lost his appetite,
Never lost his sleep at night,
Excepting one, or two, or three;

> But the loss
> Of the dollars and the land,
> Was a cross.
> Never speculate without your cash in hand.

๑๑๑

Martha's Message.

UPON the highways of Judea's plain,
   Far from the cottage of low Bethany,
Raising the dead and making the lame
To leap and praise God o'er the hills and the plain,
   And make men rejoice from sea unto sea;

Bidding the hopeless no longer to roam,
   Proclaiming glad tidings to rich and to poor;
Unto all nations salvation is come,
The widows and orphans in him find a home,
   Beyond this world's sorrows a heavenly shore.

'Tis the Master of glories, the balm of the soul,
   Whose blood was a ransom for old Adam's sin;
And happy the man who reaches the goal,
The Master prepared as the hope of the soul,
   And row their frail little boats safely in.

In Bethany Mary had watched the day go,
   As Lazarus in his lowly cot lay,
And breathed out his life calm anguish of woe,
His sister must certainly, certainly know
   The life of her brother would end with that day.

The message was sent to the Master that morn,
   That he whom thou lovest is verily ill;

Who could believe that a loved one would scorn,
Or wait for a time when a summons of harm,
  Had told him assuredly, thy brother is ill.

The sisters were waiting to see that dear face;
  Were looking and longing and weeping as well,
Should the blest Master come they were looking for
    grace,
They knew that their sorrows would vanish apace,
  And rivers of joy tumultuously swell.

Their brother had died, was buried four days,
  They weep and they mourn and the Jews sympa-
    thize.
In the small charnel house corrupting he lays,
He hears not a sound of their sad wailing ways,
  And hovering o'er him bright wings of the skies.

Some one had told them the Master was coming;
  Martha arose and went out to meet him,
She heard birds sing and e'en the bees humming
Her sorrow, yet joy, at the hope of his coming,
  Till she reached the blest spot and looked up to
    greet him.

"Dear Master," she said, "I am glad Thou hast come,
  For we have had sorrows while Thou wast away,
For Oh, Thou well knowest wherever we roam,
Our brother, Thou lovest, is not at our home,
  The angel of death has taken away."

"But, Martha, fear not, thy brother shall rise,"
  "I know he shall rise again at the last day,"
"I am that rising and any who give
Their faith to that rising shall certainly live,
  In that beautiful land far away."

Martha arose and leaving the Master,
  Believing the words that fell from his tongue;
Her steps were full firm and lighter and faster,
The birds sang a song of heavenly grandeur,
  She heard the angels with harps full and strong.

She paused at the door ere she entered the room,
  Her heart gently swelled as angels could see.
There seemed scarce a trace of sadness and gloom,
She spoke to her sister in the doorway of home,
  "The Master is come and calleth for thee."

Youth, in the pages of science or history,
  In poetry's gleam or wars for the free,
There's never a call tho' deeper the mystery,
Of half of the worth of Lazarus' sister,
  "The Master is come and calleth for thee."

Maid, tho' thy cheeks are the roses of Eden,
  And eyes sparkle bright with innocent glee,
Tho' sweet is thy voice as the cookoo at even',
Tho' many invite thee, still Martha is pleading,
  "The Master is come and calleth for thee."

❧❧❧

Hagar and Ishmael.

A GLOOMY, dreary waste of land,
    Where civil man had seldom trod,
  Where blows the wild wind o'er the sand,
    Or where the wild, tall thistles nod.

  Along its border mountains lay,
    And on their crest few feet have trod,

And at their base no brooklets play;
   No shepherd wields a shepherd's rod,

No verdant trees a refuge bring
   To stay the high noon's sultry beat;
Save rocks, that to the mountains cling,
   Naught shades the weary from the heat.

And from the caves the serpent crept,
   Or from the rocks the lion sprung;
And prey, that for his appetite
   To satiate, its life was wrung.

And near the time of setting sun,
   When mountains high a gloom o'ercast,
A mother and a child had come
   For refuge from a desert blast.

The mother wore a servant's garb,
   Her face had trace of trouble sore.
No coming night would her disturb,
   Or danger grieve her sad heart more.

The bread that on her shoulder lay,
   The bottled water 'neath her arm:
'Twas all she had her life to stay,
   And none but God to keep from harm.

She feared not for her own relief,
   But loving, as all mothers are,
She took his welfare to be chief,
   And gave to him all needed care.

The sun soon sank within the west,
   And Ishmael near her on the ground;
The mother praying earnestly,
   While piercing wildness roared around.

But God who hears the ravens cry,
   And sees the sparrows as they fall,
Will guide poor mortals with his eye,
   And keep them from the evils, all.

And He had said Who cannot lie,
   The child shall be a father, too,
And children bless him ere he die,
   And give him joy as children do.

The night was o'er, the morning sun,
   Arose from out the eastern gates,
And Hagar smiled as day begun,
   For the relief that light creates.

The beasts of prey all hid away,
   The light was more than they could bear;
For evils all from light will flee,
   That blest assurance God is there.

She looked upon the child again,
   His pleasant dreams provoked a smile.
A new love rose then for her son,
   And tears were streaming all the while.

The child arose and asked for bread;
   Since yesterday no food he had.
She felt a horrid inward dread,
   But gave the morsel to the lad.

Day came and went; their scanty food
   At last was gone, and they alone;
And Hagar rose and weeping stood,
   Beside her prostrate, dying son.

For full three days no drink he got,
   No food had touched his youthful lips;

And scorched with desert sun full hot,
  In dreams, delirious, nectar sips.

And, O, what horror filled the hour!
  While lying in the silent shade;
The draught has but insipid power,
  And by his dreams is dreadful made.

"I'll go away," she gently said,
  "That I may never see him die,
And placid he will be when dead."
  And he was left alone to die.

She slightly raised her downcast eyes,
  Her lids with sorrow drooping sore;
One loving glance cast to the skies,
  One sigh that pierced her young heart's core.

And walking slowly o'er the sand,
  Her heart with anguish broke anew;
And but for that almighty Hand,
  The outcast serf had perished too.

Not many steps from where he lay,
  She cast herself upon a rock;
And earnest for the child did pray,
  To save her from the horrid shock.

Her words were gentle, peaceful, calm;
  But, O, the cadence that they had,
Described full well the needed balm,
  So patient, gentle, fervent, sad.

'Twas thus she prayed: "Thou Holy One,
  That rulest all things whatsoe'er,
Now, condescend to save my son;
  O, great Jehovah, hear my prayer."

And from the higher courts above,
  A seraph came and heard her prayer;
He bore a message of God's love,
  And blessed her intercession there.

৵৵৵

Antitheses.

THE wonders of a fairy queen,
  Within the lone and shady dell,
Where laughs the owlet full serene,
  And where the sparkling dewdrops swell,
    Are oft to fancy's vision best;
But truer things than these I ween,
  Arise within the human heart,
And give a cadence seldom seen,
  In fancy's dream, and fancy's dart,
    And lead us to a better rest.

In youthful days we sometimes hear,
  A song by fairest mortals given,
And dream them angels hovering near,
  Just on the border land of Heaven,
    When so enraptured by the lay;
But when we pass to fullgrown years,
  And reap the cares earth holds in store,
Those songs will fill our eyes with tears,
  And give a solace and no more,
    And fairy dreamland pass away.

The beauty of the bright May morn,
  When smiles the sun upon the lea,
When hill and glen of darkness shorn,

Are casting love-smiles to the sea,
   'Tis then we merry grow and sing;
But when the bright things pass away,
   And darkness o'er the hills are come,
We only smile in hope of day,
   Or sing because we're going home,
     And borrowed all the joys we bring.

The grandeur of the angel throng,
   In Paradise so far away,
When 'round the throne they sing their song,
   Throughout the blest Eternity,
     Is oft a solace to the heart;
But when these earthly friends are dear,
   And beauties smile upon this shore,
And seem so blessed and so near,
   We want them with us evermore,
     And dreadful sorrow 'tis to part.

The grain now sown will soon be ripe,
   The harvest gathered good or ill,
The tares will hinder, causing strife,
   But let us do the Master's will,
     T' improve the talent God has given;
And when our sheaves all golden are,
   Just gathered by a weary hand,
We see the Master's smile afar,
   On glory-bordered Aiden land,
     Those golden sheaves we'll bear to Heaven.

In the Schoolhouse o'er the Way.

O MEMORY paints the scenes again,
    Which earlier years had known;
And to my heart a sad refrain,
    Has to a pleasure grown;
To dwell upon those happy hours,
    We had in childish play,
Will give the joy that oft was ours,
    In the schoolhouse o'er the way.

But when I wake to find that they,
    Are gone forevermore,
A deep regret will come to me,
    As oft it has before;
But yet those dreams so pleasant are,
    They carry joy to me,
And many benefits I gain,
    Of the schoolhouse o'er the way.

How oft our joyous shout would ring,
    The trees and buildings near
Reverberate; ten thousand times
    That sound would strike the ear;
And it was always musical,
    We heard it every day;
We dwelt upon the tone full long,
    In the schoolhouse o'er the way.

We had our little sweethearts, too,
    And love kept up the strain;
Our hearts would beat with joy each morn,

When we thus met again,
Our hearts were pure and happy then,
　When in our childish play,
We swung our sweethearts, pretty girls,
　In the schoolhouse o'er the way.

Some now are gone to distant lands,
　The toil of this life given;
And other forms are in the grave,
　Their spirits are in heaven,
A little remnant still is left,
　That meets me day by day,
But not as when we used to meet
　In the schoolhouse o'er the way.

‰

The Return to Church.

I WAS off to meetin', wife,
　In the house just o'er the way,
That modest, plain old temple—
　'Twas there I was to-day.
There's not a steeple on it, wife,
　It's built more like a barn
In which they stable cattle,
　To keep them safe and warm.

And when I looked upon it, wife,
　I thought of one of old,
T'was born within a stable,
　There sheltered from the cold.
If ever one was humble—

That is, if I can see—
That little one was humble
    On the plains of old Jude'.

An' when I went to meetin', wife,
    An' saw them faded walls,
A feelin' much consolin'
    Within my bosom crawls.
I felt a feelin' risin'
    An' givin' joy to me,
As to the cleans'ed leper
    On the shores of Galilee.

That happiness was peaceful
    An' mighty as the sea.
I knew it come from Him who trod
    The shores of Galilee.
An' much I tho't of charity
    Upon this Sabbath morn,
An' while the people sung an hymn,
    Resolved "to stand the storm."

An' then I tho't of Deacon A,
    Who cheated Neighbor M,
An' almost choked my good resolve
    Than fellowship with him.
"Fur could a fellow cheat," said I,
    "An' be a christian, too?
I'd rather build an outside shed
    An' 'fight my warfare thro'.' "

But then I tho't again, dear wife,
    'Twas very plain to see,
The Master had a Devil, too,
    In the church of old Jude'.

An' then the Master bars the gates
  Upon the other shore,
An', blessed consolation, there
  They'll bother us no more.

The meetin' was enlightenin', wife,
  My heart rose in my breast—
There's much to tell, but surely, wife
  I ne'er can tell the rest.
I wondered why I never went
  To meetin' ere this day,
For there they drop so many words
  To cheer us on our way.

I want to go to meetin', wife,
  You know the meetin's near,
An' try with all my powers, wife,
  To read my titles clear.
An' if the Scriptur's all a fib,
  As some would have appear,
I'd practice all its sayin's, wife,
  Fur the good that it does here.

The sermon bein' ended, wife,
  It gave me much of good;
The preacher left off flourishin',
  An' sentimental food;
The congregation sounded   `
  That good an' solemn hymn,
"Am I a soldier of the cross,
  A follower of the Lamb."

I felt myself a new recruit,
  An' took my shield an' sword,
An' then began a drillin'
  For the battles of the Lord.

An' in the few short hours, wife,
 I've had a fight or two,
But I'll not "fear to own his cause,"
 An' fight my warfare thro'.

It was my trait to grumble, wife,
 An' hold to every cent,
You know it all yourself, dear wife,
 It was a natural bent.
An' sometimes I would swear, wife,
 An' curse my fellow men,
An' disrespect the Holy One,
 An' take His name in vain.

I was not always honest, wife,
 I'd tell a silent lie,
By showin' all the good to sell,
 An' all the bad to buy.
So this will be my battle, wife,
 To try to cheat no more,
To love my neighbors as myself,
 An' gain a heavenly shore.

❧❧❧

The Old Cucumber Vine.

I'VE many an old, old treasure,
 In memory's storehouse stale;
And many as sweet as honey,
 Whose sweetness never fail;
But of all the good old keepsakes,
 I hold as treasure mine,

Is the withered, faded, leaflets,
   Of the old cucumber vine.

'Twas once I sat in twilight,
   As happy as a lark,
Beneath the veiling trellis,
   Which made it rather dark;
I spoke in lowest accent,
   That blessed autumn time—
O, come again, sweet picture
   Of the old cucumber vine.

But well you know the story,
   For I was not alone;
'Tis over and I care not,
   To whom the picture's shown.
'Twas Isabel the other,
   Consented to be mine,
That autumn evening twilight,
   'Neath the old cucumber vine.

Now Johnny, Ned and Mary,
   Know nothing of the place,
But Isabel comes to me,
   When I look on Mary's face;
A sweet lass of ten summers,
   She's Isabel's and mine,
But now how sad the thought is,
   Of the old cucumber vine.

Yes, Isabel has left me,
   Has left me sad and lone;
With two good boys and Mary,
   But Isabel is gone;
How sadly sweet the mem'ry,

That blissful autumn time,
Where I won a glad, devoted heart,
'Neath the old cucumber vine.

ᴊᴊᴊ

Little Lollie.

IT WAS a day in autumn late,
  When all the flowers were dead;
The lowering snow clouds hung aloft,
  And showered on our heads,
Its feathery flakes of brightest snow,
  So pure and white and dry,
They seemed by angels dropped to clothe
  The earth in purity.

And many days have passed since then,
  For, ah! 'twas years ago;
The little mound upon the hill,
  Where oft we loved to go,
Was whited o'er with winter's snow,
  And sodded o'er with green,
Full many a time, and yet her form
  Is in my vision seen.

How oft I see her bright, blue eyes
  Look up into my face,
As oft she did in years agone,
  With such a modest grace,
And then I hear her gentle voice
  A lisping unto me,
A morning greeting kindly said,
  In sweetest purity.

Full forty morns I met her thus,
  Within the schoolroom door;
The village child was fond of her,
  The aged loved her more.
They saw within her modest eyes
  A beam of heavenly light;
Her soul so pure, she seemed to be
  An angel in their sight.

But now the day, that bitter day,
  Our joy from us was riven;
And while we wept the angels, fair,
  Were singing up in Heaven.
And I can fancy that I hear
  Her little voice arise,
And greet the angels at the gate
  Of far off Paradise.

They laid her in a casket white,
  And through the churchyard door,
Four stalwart men so silently
  This faded flower bore;
And while we looked upon her face,
  Which death had turned so pale,
The tears would gush from out our eyes,
  And form a crystal vale.

We saw them lay her in the tomb,
  We heard the parson pray;
We saw them cover up her form
  With fragments of the clay;
We saw them heap the little mound,
  And smooth the surface o'er,
To point the spot in days to come,
  Where lays that gem of yore.

The village people went away,
　We left her there alone,
And in the future angels, fair,
　Will roll away the stone—
The stone that hides her little form
　Away from mortal eyes—
In beauty clothed will she come forth
　To greet us in the skies.

♪ ♪ ♪

Edwy and Elgiva.

A WAY over yonder across the deep sea,
　　Where riseth the mountains enclosing the glen;
Where patriots are wielding the arm of the free,
　And mothers are training their sons to be men.

'Tis the isle of Great Britain, the home of our sires,
　The land where the queen in her majesty reigns,
On the throne of her father's with earnest desires,
　To free all her subjects from evil disdain.

The queen on whose domain the sun never sets,
　And darkness but covers the half of her land,
All races her subjects, not one e'er regrets,
　She girdles the world with her powerful hand.

But centuries before this when Freedom was young,
　When lords lived in castles that seemed but a den,
When tyranny reigned and of charity sung,
　When christians were devils, O friends, who were
　　men?

When ruled the great terror of church over state,
  The church not from heaven its mandates did bring
But vile men of Satan corruptions create,
  And enter the churches to praise and to sing.

There rose a young ruler, a noble young king;
  One evening they crowned him in gorgeous array;
The banquet long lasted, the palace did ring
  With fair maiden voices, and youth's laughter gay.

The wine in the goblet glowed beautiful red,
  Which merry ones tasted and merrier grew,
And all were as gay as the lambs in the mead,
  Where sparkled the sunlight in silvery dew.

King Edwy was weary of church and of state
  And early retired to seek his fair queen,
For trouble assailing will love consummate,
  Or terminate joys in a vision serene.

But shadows came over the faces of those,
  Whose dancing and singing so cheery had seemed,
And fair maiden faces, with cheeks as the rose,
  Seemed waiting, as light from the chandelier
    gleamed.

The king had departed and left them alone,
  Then murmured they all at decorum so ill;
The ruby, red wine turned their feelings to stone,
  And gave them the passions that devils instill.

Loud cries for King Edwy rang out in the hall,
  And Dunstan, the abbot, determined to go,
And bring for the people who raised the loud call
  His majesty person like villainous foe.

Now Dunstan the keys of the treasury bore
  And took from the people their taxes and rent;

This power was given by Edred before,
   And Dunstan well knew that this power was spent.

And like the base ruffian when cornered by men,
   Resorts while despairing to efforts more bold,
This thief of the treasury, the basest of them,
   Confronts the young king with disgrace manifold.

So into the chamber rushed boldly the man,
   And dragged the young king from his bower of
     ease,
He sought to degrade him by boldness of plan,
   But Dunstan was banished beyond the fair seas.

The king had contentment in honeymoon joys,
   And scarce looked he off at the clouds gathering
     o'er,
But had he just turned him toward the dark skies,
   And saw the sharp lightning and heard thunders
     roar.

But kings being boys are boys in king's stead,
   Not rank, wealth or title can make them be more,
Yet noble this boy had noble ones led
   But none were so noble in wisdom or lore.

Now Dunstan was banished and Edwy was gay,
   And often at even' as shadows grew long,
He sang as a lover 'neath bowers of May,
   Of Elgiva, his fair one, this glad evening song :

            ✄

"Light of the eventide, fair and serene,
   Soft is thy mellow light tingeing the green,
Brightly the mornings be buoyant and gay,
   Softly the even light passeth away.

"Light of the eventide, come thou again,
  Shed thy sweet beauty o'er hillslope and glen,
Give to Elgiva thy soft golden light,
  Make her an angel, fair, just for to-night.

"She the most beautiful earth ever has given,
  Come then, thou mellow light, softly from Heaven,
Then will the angels be not fair as she,
  Come, little rays of light, quickly for me.

"Light of the eventide, close of the day,
  Softly thy mellow light passeth away,
Soon will the night come on o'er world and lea,
  And little breezes sweep up from the sea.

"When thou are gone away far 'neath the sea,
  Then will my lady sleep peaceful as thee,
But when thou comest again youthful and gay,
  Then will Elgiva rise blessing the way."

*

But clouds now soon gathered and shut out the sun,
  Adversity's thunder rang out deep and wild,
Intolerant lightning, to devastate, run
  His murderous darts at the poor undefiled.

For Otto, the bishop, now took up the cause,
  And stole fair Elgiva from kindred away,
And far up in Scotland, by savage outlaws,
  This beauty was taken debased wretchedly.

Elgiva returning soon met her sad fate,
  They put her in prison shut out from all day,
The song-birds of beauty this story relate,
  They heard from the prison this pitiful lay:

"Dear Edwy, come and save me,
  For I am doomed to die;
They closed me in a dungeon
  To weep and groan and sigh.
And all night long I suffered
  From pain their torture gave;
If it were not for Edwy,
  Sweet rest would be the grave.

"I long to share thy trouble;
  I long to bear my part,
For we are knit together,
  With strong cords of the heart.
And thou wouldst die to save me,
  But stolen from thy side,
Thou knowest not where to find me,
  Who last year was thy bride.

"Oh, may the angels guard thee,
  And bless thee day by day,
And give thee strength and comfort,
  Upon thy weary way.
The Holy Virgin keep thee,
  From torture and from pain,
And give thee back thy glories,
  And thy loved one again.

"But vanity my prayers be,
  And I have prayed in vain;
Soon will this mortal body,
  Be numbered with the slain;
I know they're coming, Edwy,
  I hear the rattling cart;
They'll rack me till the coldness,
  Shall pierce my aching heart.

"And when they look upon me,
   They'll laugh to scorn my plea;
And call me base and sinful,
   Because I joined with thee.
But I'll not curse them, never,
   I'll weep and pray and sigh,
Until the seraphs bear me
   Up to a world on high.

"If I could see thee smiling,
   As thou wast wont to do
Once when I sat beside thee,
   And tho't thee brave and true,
This cross would then be easy;
   This burden then be light:
And then, I'd bid thee kindly,
   My own, my sweet, good night."

*

And then the birds sighed and lowered their song,
   Till all that was heard was the breeze from the deep;
But how the queen died has never been known,
   The villain has kept it as guilty ones keep.

When Edwy had heard of the blow that was given,
   He covered in sackcloth and wept for the dead;
And sat down alone 'neath the blue vault of Heaven,
   Then raising his voice in sorrow he said:

*

"Thou art gone for aye, I hear thee not
As once I did, my fair Elgiva;
Thy sparkling eyes shall look to me,
Within my castle walls no more;

And yet I hear thy voice in dreams,
Whispering thy happy joys to me
Again, and now I feel and know,
Thrice tenfold more thy beauty.
Rather would I be a rustic youth
Among the snow-clad Scottish hills,
Than reign without thee, gentle dove,
Ta'en rudely from thy hallowed nest,
And made to bear those cruel pains,
And die the death of ignominy.
Last night I dreamed I saw thee, fair,
Within the castle walls; I heard
Thy voice in rapture sing those songs,
I used to hear thee sing so oft.
And Dunstan, too, was there and seemed
To give thee royal precedence;
He heard thee sing thy merry song,
And sat entranced as one asleep;
And when thou ceased he clapped his hands
And burst forth in a loud applause,
'Twas then I thought of happy things,
Such as I never tasted full,
Since when a romping noisy boy
I wandered o'er the summer hills.
But when my joys had made me laugh
And once I seemed a merry king,
Then I awoke; 'twas then I wished
That Heaven had not the empty dream
Confirmed to me; but rather live
A prosy life than dream a dream
All of deceit.
                 Some sunny morn,
When lifted by the joyous rays
From out my sorrow's cell, I know

'Twill be a dream, and when I wake
I'll die, my neck shall lay across
 The headsman's block, my soul shall feel
The awful shock to die.   Great God!
Are these thy servants firm and true,
And do they justly work for thee?
No, no; I'll not condemn them now
Bu t go to thee, my fair Elgiva,
Where we another crown are given.
There we'll compare and see and know,
That banes of earth bring joys in Heaven."

The sun had sunk lowly when Edwy arose,
  The grass and the treetops seemed shedding their
          tears;
The la mbs in the meadow had gone to repose,
  All solemn cadence that fell on his ears.

Tho' few were his days in this bright world of ours,
  After this sorrow, the chief of earth's woes,
He never seemed merry, the charmer's soft powers
  Could never have soothed him or given repose.

He sinks from our sight in those mystical years,
  He lost all his power by tyranny's plan,
And few of his virtues the modern world hears,
  Being lost to us all by the weakness of man.

So lost to the Britons and lost to the world
  And thrust to the grave the wise and the gay,
But what is now hidden will then be unfurled,
  When over the river the mists roll away.

Etrulia.

THE sun had risen o'er the hills,
  The birds disturbed the air so still,
  And in the distant verdant mead,
  The quiet cow, the useful steed,
  The goat that climbs the mountain height,
  Are all so tranquil in the light,
  Of glorious day, that seemed to be
  A blessing to humanity.

Across the little woodland green,
Across the little brooklet stream,
Where sang the whippoorwill at eve,
And where the cowslips fragrance leave,
But not far hence a cottage stands,
Quite near the open prairie lands;
In front the rustic woodbine twine,
And 'round the door the ivy vine.

A little spring of water, bright,
Comes bubbling up in pearly light,
Near where the little cottage stands,
Unsoiled by rude, imperfect hands.
The waters of that dainty stream
Go sparkling onward as a dream,
Until the laughing waters poured
Near where a little cascade roared.

And when the waters near the steep
Seemed pausing o'er the ledge to leap,
The morning sun that shone afar
Was caught and held in embrace there.

The little birds would fly around;
In ecstacies dart to the ground,
Or skim the waters, which the sun
Had left his coat of brightness on.

The sparkling waters would not dwell,
Full twenty fathoms down they fell,
And, up the steep no feet could climb,
On either side straight as a line,
The rocks were piled so huge and square
The mountain goat was baffled there.
Thus for a mile this ravine deep
No creature climbed, it was so steep.

How forth the little brooklet main
Went sparkling in the open plain,
How farther went, I do not know,
Nor, care I, for its onward flow.
But, to the little cot once more,
Where lies the watch-dog on the floor;
A bushy, manteled dog was he,
With many a trait of charity.

The inmates of that little home,
Were three, who always sat alone,
While evening hearth was burning bright,
And antiquated lamps, the light,
By which they sewed, by which they read,
By which they ate their daily bread;
And very happy were the three,
Whose sighs or murmurs ne'er could be.

The man, the wife, the child, 'twas three,
Whose smile had alway seemed to be;
And not a cloud of trouble rose,
To mar their peace, as I suppose,

For many a year until this morn
In June, when verdant was the corn,
And gay the flowers within the plot,
Where grew the bright forget-me-not.

The child, a little maiden, fair,
With hazel eyes and auburn hair,
With lips so sweet, and cheeks so red,
Her form so agile as she sped
The little path, each morn and eve,
To guide the cattle, and to leave
Them on the lea or at the gate,
At early morn or evening late.

She had not passed bright summers o'er,
Than half a score, not less or more,
And in the glen she oft would glide,
With faithful Rover by her side;
And when she passed the birds would sing,
The rabbits leap, and all would ring,
With notes of joy, so happy they,
Because the maiden passed that way.

The father loved the little girl,
Not for her eyes or auburn curl,
But for the noble heart within,
So many joys to him had been.
The mother loved as mothers do;
She thought no heart so good and true;
And if, at even, she staid late
Her mother worried at the gate.

And oft the father, cane in hand,
Would go beyond the timber land,
And list to hear her youthful song,
Or looked to see her glide along,

And oft she met him light and gay,
And laughing fast would glide away,
And meet her mother at the gate,
Who censured mild for staying late.

And while Etrulia older grew,
And to her parents dearer too;
I sometimes think that Heaven saw
The wily tempter from Him draw,
And chastened them to bring them back,
And guide them in the blissful track.
But what it was that caused it so,
It ne'er has been my lot to know.

And on that morn the sun was bright,
The day seemed just as full of light
As any day that had passed by.
The robin's song, the clear blue sky,
With not a cloud of dark or gray;
None gave a token of the day—
The day that clips the bright, gay flower,
And glomifies the passing hour.

Forth from the cot the little maid,
Now glided through the morning shade;
Her eyes were glistening in the light,
Her song was gay, her smile was bright;
Her flowing curls of hair full hung,
And sparkled bright in the morning sun;
And not a shadow wrought her brow,
And not a care was burden now.

And so Etrulia glided on,
Glad in the bright light of the sun,
Just as she oft before would glide,
With faithful Rover at her side.

Now sang the little birds in trees,
And hummed the little busy bees,
And then the flowers seemed to smile,
At gay Etrulia all the while.

And passing on they neared the steep;
Within the rocks the serpents creep,
And never show their envious head,
Until they strike their victim dead,
Save to alarm, when well they clasp,
Their death-doomed victim in their grasp.
But serpents are not all that kill,
E'en with the monster of the still.

And well Etrulia serpents dread,
And knew full well the life they led;
And just as well the fate she knew,
Of one whose veins their poison drew.
But guarded well Etrulia went,
Her bounding heart would ne'er repent,
Of carelessness, that is such care,
That guarded 'gainst the serpents' snare.

Now in this world there sometimes seem,
That youthful forms think life a dream,
Without a care, or wily snare,
So innocent; and oft the glare
Of Satan's form, like angels seem,
Allures them off.   They know they dream;
And dreaming so they ne'er are free,
And live to dream and not to be.

They dream and so dream on all night,
For surely life devoid of light,
Has been to them.   They know they dream,
And try to wake, but not a gleam

Of real life to them is given,
Save what repentance gets in Heaven.
Oh! be it humble, be it poor,
Regard the real pathway more.

Etrulia knew full well the trap,
That serve the useful ones, to sap,
Of usefulness.   Her parents taught
Her of this way of danger fraught,
And bade her wake and know the truth,
And not go dreaming in her youth,
And so Etrulia could not well,
Be led astray by that vile spell.

But as the spiders wily be,
And set their trap in corner sly,
The Prince of Hades sets his trap,
And looks his fiendish eyes thereat,
And laughs a laugh to me it seems
I oft have heard in evil dreams.
And then transformed the evil one
Allures his harmless victim on.

Now near the path so smooth and worn,
Etrulia went each eve and morn,
O'erhanging quite the ravine deep,
A little mound of earth full steep
Where never foot of man had trod,
To start the ground or mar the sod;
And on the mound a flower grew,
For beauty 'twas excelled by few.

Etrulia paused; she saw the flower,
She looked again, and in her power
She thought it was to pluck and keep,
To make a bouquet fragrant, sweet;

'Twas near the ledge, ah, well she knew,
The feet that walked thereon were few,
And she was small. She knew that men
Would never dare that point to gain.

"I'll try" she said, and smiled the while,
There seemed a glory in that smile;
And tossing back her flowing hair,
See trilled a tra-la in the air.
She sang not knowing 'twas the last
That she should sing. The light o'ercast
Her smiling form with golden hue,
As oft reflecting light will do.

She cautiously went up the steep,
She saw the waters overleap
The precipice, and then to flow
On, laughingly, so deep below.
She saw the mosses on the walls,
So straight they seemed, and at the falls,
She saw a deer stoop down and drink
While standing on the brooklet brink.

She glanced at them a moment and
The borders seemed like glory land,
All things seemed then with joy o'ercast,
Now look, sweet maiden, 'tis your last,
The hours are past that have an end,
That to thy vitals substance lend,
And if thou singest, thou singest for aye,
In that brighter world of day.

The horror of that dreadful hour,
The wiliness of Satan's power,
That God the fallen angel lends,
And strive to make the parent's friends,

Is given.   The beauty of the summer days,
The music of the robin's lays,
Will cheer their smitten hearts no more,
And only God can heal the sore.

And holding to the shrub, she drew
Up near the little flower to,
Sweet innocence that smileth now,
And blusheth still with youthful glow,
Thy charms stay not the evil hand,
Thy song shall cease in all the land,
In days to come will many be,
Who oft will sigh and think of thee.

Now, with a little muffled groan,
And to her ears a fearful tone,
The earth gave way beneath her feet,
And she was left her doom to meet.
But not an ear was there to hear,
Save birds of song no help was near.
Oh, awful doom, thus every word,
And every dying groan unheard!

Etrulia fell.   Reflecting light
Was shining on her form full bright,
And where those hazel eyes once danced,
And many kind affections glanced,
Were covered o'er, as if asleep.
And, now, her parents would not weep,
At seeing her so pure and calm,
As if asleep within the glen.

But, clusters of disheveled hair,
O'erlaid her form of beauty there,
And when the hunter came that way,
And seeing Etrulia prostrate lay,

His mind reverts to fairyhoods,
Of sleeping beauty in the woods,
And drawing close he gently said,
"It is Etrulia, sleeping?   Dead!"

.l..l..l.

The Two Sons.

DEAR wife, I'm feeling sad to-day,
    My tho'ts revert once more
To brighter times and brighter days
    Upon this transient shore;
And then, returning, follow up
    The weal mixed with the woe,
I think 'tis very queer and strange
    How blindly people go.
When we were young, dear wife, you know
    I had a forward way,
And always very positive,
    What I should do and say.

And you remember father's hut,
    That stood down by the lane;
Well, I was there to-day, dear wife,
    And 'twas a sad refrain.
The old hut stands, but 'tis decayed,
    The doors and windows out,
The weeping willow by its side,
    Where once we heard the shout
Of gleesome, playing children, wife,
    And I would join the lay,
When singing little songs we knew
    Upon a summer day.

And as I sat within the shade
  O' th' dear old willow tree,
It joined me in the sad refrain,
  The memory of our glee.
And as I stepped within the door,
  All things seemed sacred there,
For 'round the old hearth in the morn
  We often said our prayer;
But the boards are rotting where we knelt,
  The brick torn from the hearth;
The shade is still on summer days
  Devoid of childish mirth.

I tho't of all my youthful days,
  And tears began to fall;
And of the little love I had
  For Him who gave me all;
And oh, how often I regret
  The cruel words I said.
And oft in anger words of shame
  Were heaped on father's head,
And those poor loving lips were dumb
  In angry words to me,
And then, in accents kind and mild,
  They often pleadingly
Would pray for me on the dear old hearth,
  Just at the dawn of day—
We never know a treasure's worth
  Till it is gone away.

And father, wife, was kind to me,
  But I was not to him;
A disobedient, wilful son,
  Rife with many a sin.
He tried to plead with me for right,

He tried to tell me then,
That he was old and I was young,
    As one day he had been,
That I was young, in years to come
    That I should older grow,
That some day I might learn to feel
    The limits of his woe.

"The Bible's true."   His words were calm,
    It makes my heart now bleed;
"And he who sows in youthful days,
    In old age reaps the seed."
And I distinctly recollect
    Just where my father stood,
Beneath the shady cherry tree,
    Close by the little wood;
And oh, that spot was sad to me
    When I was there to-day,
I seem to hear those fatal words
    From dreamland far away.

And I forgot that I was old
    In my excited fears,
I would have run, but then my limbs
    Had stiffened with the years.
The wicked surely never live
    Out half their numbered days,
For tho' I live I'm certain still
    I'm dead in many ways.

And there are John and James, my boys,
    You know, wife, how you weep,
And many, many nights of pain
    You pass in troubled sleep,
Because our sons use unkind words,

Speak roughly without shame,
And think no harm to say, "Old man,
  Pick up your hat and cane."
You know 'tis true my trembling hand
  And tottering footsteps bring
Full many a mishap to my boys,
  And then the curses ring.
But I can scarcely blame them, wife,
  Thus fate has brought along,
For this I did when I was young,
  I did when I was young.

At breakfast time, one morning, wife,
  You know when I sat down,
My nervous hand the coffee spilled
  Upon that young wife's gown;
And then her husband, my dear son,
  Spoke up with cruel tone
And said: "Old chap, I'll have you eat
  With hogs, who better grown,
Will not insult their fellow hog
  In such an awkward way."
But wife, I'm quite resigned to this,
  I'll only trust and pray,
And feel that God is sending me
  The harvest good and strong,
For thus I sowed when I was young,
  I sowed when I was young.

So I've been telling James and John
  All that was told to me,
And plead with them for Jesus' sake,
  But they never heed my plea.
Their few short years they think 's enough
  To know more than I know;

They dote on things of little worth
  And aggravate me so;
But many years of toil and strife
  Teach me to hold my peace,
And wait until my summons comes
  My spirit to release.
I hope and pray that they may see
  That they are surely wrong,
Look not, like me, when they are old,
  To days when they were young.

Dear wife, cease now to shed your tears,
  I think my sad days o'er,
For God forgives my early sins
  Committed, days of yore.
I have the good old church, dear wife,
  Within the quiet shade;
I'd rather kneel with saints of God,
  Than stand with honor's blade;
You know I used to say "'tis false,"
  I tho't it foolishness,
But God hath chosen foolish things
  To banish wickedness.
But O, my sons, could you but know
  The source from which it sprung—
But I was so when I was young,
  Was so when I was young.

At Even'.

A^T EVEN' I sit and I ponder,
   I sit and I think and I dream,
Of visions of beauty; no wonder,
   For sometimes they are what they seem.

The zephyrs soft come thro' my window,
   My heart with emotion does swell;
They come as a gentle soft whisper,
   But never a word do they tell.

I hear the sweet laughter of childhood,
   And, surely, a charm them is given.
Up comes the blest words of the Master,
   "Of such is the kingdom of Heaven."

And then come the words of another,
   One noted for wisdom and lore,
Who carries this childhood in manhood,
   Enjoys this pleasant world more.

Who seeks to be kind and forgiving,
   He seeks to be righteous and wise,
Partakes of the beauty of children,
   And gets a reward in the skies.

The bell of the church is now ringing,
   So solemnly falls on my ear,
The sound of its doleful endeavor
   To bring all the wayward ones near.

Then ring, sexton, ring out the summons
   Which makes my heart solemnly swell,

You'll get your reward up in Heaven,
  By saving a soul with the bell.

But sometimes the sound is so doleful,
  It tolls the sad march to the tomb,
And joins with the cry of the mourner
  To deepen the sadness and gloom.

But, ah, for the spirit departed,
  These emblems of sadness and gloom
Are but the farewell to his sorrow,
  The portals of Heaven, the tomb.

Then toll, sexton, toll the sad parting,
  Let sorrow not enter thy breast;
Thy tolling will add for the pilgrim
  New joy to the welcome of rest.

⁂

The Prelude.

THE storm-cloud rose aloft in majesty,
  And seemed defiant in his tones of voice,
His fringing hung in dark-hued tapestry,
  His shadow gloomed the rippling of the lake.

His roaring trembled far the wide extended earth,
  And seemed to strike anon the heavenly dome,
Ere this, the air was rife with pretty mirth,
  But Providence had willed another storm.

Not yet, altho' the gloom extends afar,
  Not yet, the storm breaks from the ebon sky,
Not yet, the pelting hail the landscape mar,
  Not yet; all nature strained to stand the storm.

But oh, a stillness grand, sublime, and loud,
  Makes speeches as 'twere from Jehovah's lips,
And tells us worlds from out the summer cloud,
  But these ears of ours are much too dull to hear.

It hangs just as a little drop oft hangs,
  Beneath the petals of a morning flower;
As if to wait the jarring of a mighty hand,
  To start the falling of a mighty shower.

The prelude of the shower is o'er at last,
  It tells us much, but little of 't we know,
That little bids us look beyond the shower,
  And see a brighter sun, a fairer sky, a sweeter glow.

Weal and Woe.

Down the path of life we go,
  Laugh with joy and sigh with sorrow,
  And from out the future borrow,
What of weal and what of woe,
  Live to-day within the morrow.

Things are gladdest that are gone,
  And we weep at their sad parting,
  At the sigh and at the starting,
And we only hear their tone
  In the dreamland of the parting.

Things are saddest yet to come,
  And the veil we lift in dreaming
  Of the future has a seeming,
Of a sadder, sadder home,
  E'en if prospects bright are gleaming.

Tho' the hopes will brighter grow;
  Oft a gleam of sunshine bringing,
  And we happy go to singing;
Thus the weal, but ah! the woe
  To the heart is sadly clinging.

Blasted hopes the past has seen;
  This the more will doubt the morrow;
  Crushing love and bringing sorrow;
Fade the bloom and wilt the green
  In the doubting for to-morrow.

Thus we sadly go and sing
  In the world terrestrial ever,
  Met but only meet to sever,
Still the contrite heart will bring
  Glory joys beyond the river.

᯽᯽᯽

To a Lady.

THE little zephyrs from the west
  Now sing a little dirge to me,
And try to change my merry heart
  To be distressed because of thee.

But not a note can change me now,
  I will not list to things so weak;
I'd rather live a hermit life
  Than die of such a silly freak.

I know that thou art beautiful,
  The tresses of thine auburn hair
Do glisten as a precious gem,
  No fairy e'er was half so fair.

And then those azure eyes of thine
　　Excel by far the ether skies;
It seems that all the purest tints
　　Are concentrated in thine eyes.

Thy form, so graceful and so neat,
　　Has oft suggested unto me
A fairy dream that might have been
　　When in a closer walk with thee.

And if, when bidding thee adieu,
　　A tear should trickle unrestrained,
I'd think 'twas but the falling dew,
　　Or else the clouds a drop had rained.

Gone---Lost.

God keeps his records up in heaven,
　　And sits upon the throne;
When idle moments go he writes,
　　"Another moment gone."

When heavy is the burden borne,
　　By him, a weary one,
Thou smilest not, 'tis then he writes,
　　"Another jewel gone."

And smiles are all such golden gems,
　　A kindness gently done,
For what then should our Maker write,
　　"Another jewel gone."

And looking o'er the lives we live,
  O'er other days now flown,
How many pages witness this,
  "Another jewel gone."

And summing up the jewels bright
  In careless moments riven,
How little we accumulate
  To take with us to heaven.

♔ ♔ ♔

Reflection.

WHEN youth has formed a heart to love,
  And beauties grace the evening bower,
When starlit skies give forth their light,
  And smile upon a beauty's face;
When songs peal forth, and thrill the chord
Of that vibrating harp of life,
And make your trembling soul go forth
In weakness at her very feet;
When eyes that heavenly angels keep
Full bright with early dew of life,
Shine on you with their graceful beams,
The throbbing heart will beat aloud,
As if by some strange fairy wand
Those eyes were touched to touch the heart
And melt to love.
            So is our youth,
It comes with beams of heavenly love;
It swells our hearts to that extent—
That all we know of life or death

Is that we live and happy are.
And if our youth would always last,
What incense would these fires burn,

The cursed earth would beam with love,
And let the darkness pass away,
But youth must go.   The morning sun
Will strengthen 'till the moontide heat,
And then decline to setting sun,
All peaceful at the day's calm close,
A perfect life.
               But seldom earth
Will let good prudence lift the veil.
And show to one a perfect life;
Ah, seldom, never is too oft
For earth to grant a perfect life,
Since he who trod Judea's plain,
And wept o'er fair Jerusalem
Because he knew she would not give
Consent to share his love.
No perfect man has ever lived,
With soul ne'er stained with taint of sin
And he a God, a God in truth.
But for the great Physician's balm,
That clears the soul of infamy,
And makes it pure and white as snow,
The stricken soul is crimson dyed;
Our souls be lost for aye, for aye,
And never have a glance of day.

But O, my heart, presume not now
To dwell on things of dire all gone,
The real sorrows of this life
Are quite enough for one to bear,
Much less to think of things of naught,

That might have been.   Do not, O muse,
Aspire to delve beneath the shade
Of certain things and search for doubt;
But give thy wings full strength to dart
And shape the many things that are,
And make the sleepy lump arise,
To give sweet joy to lonely man.
But youth, the pleasant morn of life,
When first we rise to take the path,
And see all sunshine in the way;
What pleasant seas, so calm, and clear,
What rippling waves by zephyr made,
Which seem as smiles cast up to God;
What fields of flowers which rise and fall
To give the petals varied hues,
To spread the sun tints over all
And cast a golden, heavenly garb;
What giant trees the forests have
To form the heart to do great deeds,
And lofty grow up as the trees,
And standing staunch upon their base,
Resist the roaring tide of winds
That, adverse to their mighty strength,
Strive hard to lay them doubly low.
But if the heart is pure and sound,
And knows no taint of rottenness,
'Twill firmer stand and stronger grow
By adverse winds.
                    The lillies smile,
The ripples laugh and playful look
Up to the wind which onward drives;
The giant oak but roars serene,
And at the calm it gently sleeps
A solemn sleep.

So may we learn
To gather joy from out the storm,
And labor on serene and calm;
To stem the tide and stand the storm,
And God will grant a better rest
Beyond this vale of tears.

ﻙﻙﻙ

The First Christmas.

O'ER the plains of old Jude'
 Sounded forth the jubilee,
  Glorious heavenly strain;
Angels gave the joyful news,
That to the long expectant Jews
 A Holy Son was born.
A Savior of the fallen race
 Within the world was come,
And they who strive to seek his face
 Shall find in Him a home.

And when the gospel throng announced
The rife air radiant music bounced,
 And angels filled the space;
The heavenly hosts the chorus sang,
The welkin dome with music rang;
 Doubly rebound the lays.
The notes ascended beyond the skies,
 The Father heard and smiled,
And untold glories ever rise
 Around the golden throne.

Within the city Bethlehem,
Close by the village public inn,
    A lonely stable stood.
Because the inn was filled with guests,
They sought asylum with the beasts,
    This holy couple did.
The Holy Child that day was born.
    Far in the eastern sky,
His star arose long ere the morn
    It's radiant bars had riven.

With stabled beasts, a Holy Babe
Within the manger-cradle laid,
    A glorious gift of Heaven.
A high-born Savior of the world,
That day from Heaven the news unfurled,
    By wing'ed seraphs given.
And there He lay, a royal king,
    First born offspring of Heaven.
That little group some comfort bring,
    By Him their Lord new-riven.

Far in the East the star was seen,
Across Judea's fragrant green,
    That star denoted a king.
The wise men to the city went,
To seek the new-born king, intent,
    In the city Jerusalem.
Up to the city o' the Great King,
    With gifts of myrrh they come,
And inquired for a king new-born,
    To worship at His feet.

With anxious look and nervous tread,
King Herod heard, then sent with dread

A page to know the truth.
The page at temple doorway stood,
For him who knew the sovereign's good,
    The chosen people's priest.
And while he knocked the hinges turned,
  He looked and there beheld
The high priest with his incense urn,
    In full attire arrayed.

"A servant of the king I see,
A noble sovereign just to me,
    What is my master's wish?"
Then kind obeisence courtesied he,
And said, "the king's at peace with thee,
    But asketh of thee this:
To bring the chief priests and the scribes,
  Within his royal court,
To ask a question of thy tribe,
    To give his cause support."

"As is his word, so shall it be;
To hear his word is to obey
    And now I bid adieu."
"Farewell," the other said
And straightway to the palace sped.
    The priest his task in view
Then called his brethren one and all,
  Those of the priestly clue;
They meet within the judgment hall,
    Then passed within the court.

The king forgot his royal cloak,
He seemed a withe as once an oak,
    He feared a tottering throne.
He rushed into the court to hear

Where the new king was to appear,
    Fear quaking every bone.
He saw the Jewish elders fall
    Before him as he came,
He bade them rise, then asked them all;
    They told him, "Bethlehem."

Forthwith he gave the wise men word,
Would have their mission not deferred,
    He bade them all God speed,
"And further, when ye find the king,
Then the glad message to me bring,
    That I may worship, too."
They went, and lo, the guiding star
    Guided them in the way,
Which seems as yet to shine afar,
    And guide us to this day.

They found the babe in Bethlehem,
They worshiped at its feet, at them
    Their gifts they offered Him,
But ne'er returned they to the king;
They knew 'twas evil this to bring
    The tyrant word again.
For in his evil heart he thought
    To slay the blessed One.
While thro' his wisdom God had brought,
    He sheltered, too, His Son.

And thus the first glad Christmas day
Was spent by those so far away,
    The day the Child was born.
What month or day is not now known,
As learned men sufficient own,
    But well we know 'twas so.

But for this boon we need not pray,
   The day of His advent,
We'll have our Christmas every day,
   And never need repent.

⚹⚹⚹

Charity.

I WATCH thee as from soul to soul thou goest,
   And happier am, when thou art with me here;
I search thee oft; a starving soul thou knowest
   Is often feed on thy reviving tear.

I've seen kind eyes grow cold and harsh without thee;
   I've heard harsh tones thy absence well relate;
No gentler form has ever been about me,
   Tho' be they rich as Crœsus, and as great.

'Tis not the learned that know full well thy beauty,
   'Tis not the strong can hold thy spirit mild;
And they who tread the path of honest duty,
   May see thy spirit in a laughing child.

Let Caesar learn the art of war and murder,
   Let Abra'm's faith heave up the mighty sea;
Let Socrates and Plato still go farther,
   But let me be, O, gentle one, with thee.

Whate'er with wrong the harsher spirit marreth,
   And draggeth down the heart to lower spheres;
Thou cheerest yet, and for the wounded carest,
   And bindest up with pleadings and with tears.

When other spirits would let me sink in ruin,
   And conscience strong my guilty spirit quails,

While in the path of doubt and guilt pursuing,
  Thy potent hand, in lifting, never fails.

Decaying Lazarus may feel thy quickening power,
  And Zacheus haste to humble where thou art,
Bethesda's pool, all hail the healing hour,
  Tho' Jews despise, with Satan, do their part.

Thou hearest the cry of those who bent in sorrow,
  And watchest, too, the sparrow as it falls,
And findest joy to hope on each to-morrow,
  Tho' on to-day the crushing sorrow calls.

The widow's cry makes rife the morning breezes,
  The noonday sun brings to her no relief;
Thy gentle spirit, her of a burden eases,
  And changed to joy what were without thee grief.

And he who walks within the path of duty,
  And heareth wisdom as she cries to him,
May yearn the presence of the blessed beauty,
  And yearn thy power, the antidote for sin.

The young may rise and with thy power prosper,
  The old retain much beauty of their youth,
And e'en in death I know that thou wilt whisper,
  "There's joy beyond, then hope thou in the truth,"

*

To a Little Girl.

CHILDHOOD is with you now, Mary,
    Childhood so happy and gay,
  Sunshine and flowers attend you,
  Happiness gladdens your way.

Childhood will flee from you, Mary,
  Cares and afflictions will come;
Then you will long for your childhood,
  Long for your parents and home.

Tho' you may live in a palace
  Ringing with music so gay,
You never will feel half so happy
  As, Mary, you're feeling to-day.

Then, give to your parents, dear Mary,
  The kindness they to you have given;
'Twill pacify life's dreary pathway,
  'Twill gain you a home up in Heaven.

✣✣✣

Vacation.

Hark, the birds are singing
  Out on the pleasant lea,
Beasts and birds and meadow
  Now welcome you and me.
Our schoolday tasks are over,
  Our time of playing come,
We'll take a short vacation
  Within the light of home.

Our books be not forgotten,
  Our joyful play will give
A relish for their study,
  That we may learn and live.
Then let us take vacation,
  Which has no rigid rule.
When that short time be ended,
  Return with joy to school.

Autumn Roses.

THE autumn rose is coldly red,
   Shows sorrows in its beautied face,
As if for grief; glad moments sped
   Are sweeter than the present grace.

The happy springtime flowers smile
   And show no furrowed sorrow wave;
The summer flowers serenely while
   Their days along into the grave.

To me the autumn rose is here—
   Its faded crimson petals, too—
I live within the past, I fear,
   Too much my present tasks to do.

This eve I lisped my mother's name,
   In an unguarded anxiousness,
With which a cloud of sorrow came
   Because it soothed not my distress.

Because I never more shall hear
   That tender voice—I loved it so—
It passed away in autumn sear
   One sadly-solemn year ago.

But still it seems a spirit voice
   Warns me of error and of sin,
And pleads me make a nobler choice
   Than earthly transientness to win.

It comes just like it used to come,
   And makes my sad heart feel its power;

I think of mother and of home,
  Which gloomifies the passing hour.

But then it makes me happy still
  To know she ever meant it right,
And pled her wayward son to fill
  A soldier's rank in a christian fight.

While thus I muse on that dear form
  And blessed words of advice given,
I feel she now is free from harm,
  At rest with all the saints in Heaven.

Sometimes I to the churchyard go,
  And pause just by a lonely mound;
Tho' sad it makes me, yet I know
  That mother may not there be found.

Yet true I saw them place her form
  Within a grave beneath that mound,
And wept to know that she was gone
  As if they placed her in the ground.

But that was what enveloped her
  That caused her sorrow here below,
And at the mound I surely err
  To wish her as one year ago.

And with this train there flood my soul
  A thousand tender ties of home,
And often from their grave I roll
  Away the large and mossy stone.

But 'tis not there I find those ties,
  For they have changed their place with years.
Their spirit force is in the skies,
  And but their forms bring forth my tears.

And that, e'en that directs my course
   For good or ill, as it may be,
As in the little brooklet source
   Start waters for the mighty sea.

Sweet mansion! 'neath thy time-browned roof,
   What memories gather, sad, sublime,
And gild my soul with gems of truth
   That fade not with the lapse of time.

Tho' autumn rain and autumn chill
   Turn dark thy coating many a day,
Yet in those halls the spirits fill
   My soul with new-born ecstacy.

When first I learned to gaze on things
   Of transientness, tho' lovely forms;
And drink the evanescent springs
   Of childish joy so uniform.

How bright the pathway down the lane
   As memory paints the picture o'er;
As years go by they come again
   And beckon us to days of yore.

A sister's voice I used to hear
   At early morn when half asleep,
With solemn somberness so clear,
   With sweetness that I ever keep.

I ever keep in memory dear,
   For as she sung that "God is love,"
I felt that he was very near
   And knew his presence from above.

When first I caught that eye of love,
   That glowed its blessings on my head,

And learned full well its worth to prove,
　　When words of true affection said;

I knew not that in after years,
　　When sitting as I sit this eve,
Would drop some penitential tears
　　For sorrows that will never leave.

When brother in our boyhood days
　　Would clasp me in a fond embrace,
And join me in our childish ways
　　In running oft from place to place;

I tho't not of the days when we
　　Should sever far no more to meet
As we did then in perfect glee,
　　The joys of childhood days to greet.

We used to climb the orchard trees,
　　And watch the robins in their nest;
Or rob the fearless bumblebees,
　　Their well-stored honey-cups in quest.

We used to scour the the thickest wood
　　With little Fido, faithful dog,
And caught the squirrels that we could
　　By chopping from a hollow tree.

We used to with the neighbor boys
　　Engage in many a common play,
And have our share of youthful joy,
　　In winter snow or pleasant May.

And oft in springtime verdant, too,
　　We used to bring the cattle home,
That wandered far the forest thro',
　　Impelled by pasture land to roam.

We used to list to hear the bell
  That hung suspended on the neck,
To save full many a step and tell
  Their feeding place, who little reck.

And many another care had we,
  That gave us much of pleasure then,
In after years, which was to be,
  To others given for we were men.

We used to walk by the brooklet brink
  And watch the sparkling waters flow,
And on its banks I used to think
  Just as its sparkling waters flow.

And all the strains I sang those days
  Were strains of merriment and glee,
Like the pearly waters in the stream
  And the laughing warble upon the trees

But now I stand on the ocean shore;
  Within its depths I ne'er can see;
I hear its mighty billows roar,
  And they unfathomed seem to me.

After Many Days.

WHEN the twilight gathers softly,
  At the setting of the sun,
When the world is fringed with beauty;
  When the reapers' work is done;
And the birds that sang so sweetly
  All the day, have ceased to sing,

Save the robin and the linnet,
  In the trees above the spring.

When the breezes from the highland
  Gently move the opening rose;
And the daisies in the meadow
  All their petals gently close;
When the heart is ever peaceful,
  And the soul serenely blest;
When surrounded with these blessings,
  Sweet the slumber and the rest.

But the soul that knows the anguish,
  And the sorrow, and the strife,
And the many bitter trials,
  That assail us in this life,
All these blessing will not furnish
  To that weary soul a rest,
Save by faith when hearts look upward,
  To that land where dwell the blest.

While I pondered thus at even',
  O'er the pangs my heart had known,
And reclining gently slumbered—
  To the fairy dreamland shown—
And I stood beside a cottage
  Covered o'er with woodbine green,
But to mortals such a cottage,
  Save in dreamland, ne'er was seen.

Sitting near the rustic dorway,
  On a smooth and flattened stone,
With his ragged arms enfolded,
  A troubled peasant sat alone.
"Good morning, sire," I hailed him kindly;
  He looked, and smiled at what I said.

"Good morning, friend." His voice had pity
   As one a contrite life had led.

On his brow a somber paleness,
   In his eye a troubled look,
In his hand he held a volume,
   'Twas the Bible, blessed book.
Then I chanced to ask a question
   Of his troubles, how they come,
Of his labors, how he prospered,
   Then at last I asked his name.

Then his eyes assumed a luster
   I had often seen before,
In the eyes of forlorn stranger,
   Begging at your social door;
If his hope was scarcely living,
   As he spoke to you of bread,
Welcome words would then revive them,
   Thus the eyes this rustic had.

"I have labored hard for Heaven,
   Given all my stock and store,
Given up the worldly pleasure,
   Till I have to give no more;
I have labored for my fellows,
   Strengthened many a weary heart,
Till the day is almost over;
   Soon, ah, soon I must depart."

"I have gathered for my labors,
   Nothing but regret and shame,
'Tho' He slay me, still I'll trust Him,
   May be I will Heaven gain.'"
All his words with sorrow laden,
   With the burden that he bore,

But that burden shall be vanished
  Never on this mortal shore.

Many days of ceaseless labor,
  Many hours of ceaseless prayer,
Many weary hearts he lightened
  From their sorrow, from their care;
He complains of many hardships,
  Of his toil without reward;
Still he firmly, truly trusted
  In the promise of the Lord.

Then I sank into my slumber,
  Saw the peasant not again
In this mortal land of sorrow,
  In this habitat of man,
Till he came to cross the river
  For the distant, better shore,
Till he bade farewell to sorrow
  And to care forevermore.

Then I dreamed, and in my dreaming
  Saw the boatman touch the shore,
Heard the peasant whisper, "Welcome,"
  As he ne'er had lisped before.
And he bade farewell to mortals,
  Smiled and said, "I'm going home."
Few were weeping, still he soothed them,
  "Do not weep, you'll all come soon."

And he stepped in with the boatman,
  And with muffled oar they rowed,
Till they neared the farther landing
  Where the lights of Heaven glowed.
Then the angels bid him welcome
  And the harps with music rang,

And the glorious choir of Heaven
Many hallelujahs sang.

And they put a robe upon him,
    Whiter than the purest snow,
On his head a crown of glory
    Glittered with a heavenly glow,
Many stars of vict'ry shining
    As the pearly stars of night
Glittered in his crown of glory
    Like the precious diamond bright.

It was over, I was sitting
    In my easy chair again,
On the stand the light was flitting,
    And the owlet from the glen
Flew beneath my window lattice,
    Screamed along the orchard trees;
I was startled with this thrilling
    And the whistling of the breeze.

And I wandered long aweary,
    If my dream a meaning bore
Could I gain from it a lesson
    T' rectify the wrongs of yore?
This the lesson I have gathered.
    Trudging on in wisdom's ways,
I shall gain the port of Heaven
    Surely, "After many days."

A Dream.

WHAT wonders and surprises pass we thro' in this
     wide world,
  What heaps of broken promises and tho'tless sins
     unfurled,
What by-paths we have wandered in search of wealth
     or fame,
  What scars from opposition if e'er we get a name.

In youthful dreams we ponder and think of naught
     but joy,
  The girl of palace dainties, of fame and wealth the
     boy,
And in ecstatic musing our voice will ring with song,
  The swelling of the music will bear our soul along.

How often, oh, how often we see in future near,
  The blessing that this world gives upon this mun-
     dane sphere,
How often, oh, how often they think to gain a rest
  Thro' paths of ease complaisant and sit down with
     the blest.

In youthful mood serenely tho' sad its wages seem,
  While doting on this question I slept and dreamed
     a dream,
And tho' there's nothing novel in dreaming dreams
     I know,
  Yet sometimes to the dreamer instructive visions
     show.

I tho't me transformed to the border
  Of a beautiful circular hill,
Where snow falls as emblems of virtue
  And rain the depressions do fill;
I tho't I saw just at the hilltop
  And fringed with a radiant glow,
A throne stand as staunch as the rocks stand
  And white as the purest of snow.

Bright clouds surrounded the glory,
  Tho' darkly to mortals they show,
And hide from the eye of the mortals
  The light of that heavenly glow;
And angels cherubic, seraphic,
  Moved gracefully in the bright air,
And moved their bright wings with the music
  That floated so wonderful fair.

The throne in dimension was greater,
  Thrice greater than ever I saw,
To show us the strength of the Person
  Whose word is unlimited law.
Now the plain on this hillslope was grassy,
  Interspersed with beautiful flowers,
And the mortals that stood on the hillslope
  Were praising this gay world of ours.

Some were weeping and mourning in sadness
  The evil that burdened them down,
Ne'er lifted their eyes to the Heavens,
  Still the goodness of Heaven they own;
The earth has its objects too tempting,
  They glitter and glow in their eyes,
And charmed them as charmeth the siren,
  And taketh their looks from the skies.

And the angel, Compassion, wept o'er them
  And offered a bright golden crown,
And pleaded, Look up and reach forward,
  But their lookings are ever cast down.
Some said they were taking a journey
  To the ever blest fields of delight,
But, contrary, took the direction
  And ended in miserable night.

Some said that the cup was a blessing,
  And drank of its bitterest dregs,
And hurled themselves down to destruction
  In poverty, misery and rags.
But woe to that mate of the drunkard,
  And woe to the wife and the child;
More woe to the wretched dramseller,
  This sanctum his hand hath defiled.

So then in my dream 'twas I saw them,
  In pleasure they gathered their woe,
And I wept when I saw in their pathway
  To Heaven no journeyman go,
And I cried in my bitterest anguish,
  O, God, is there none that do right?
And an angel rebuked me in silence,
  O, faithless one, cease thy affright.

And I looked and I saw a lone pathway,
  With only a wanderer or two,
And I tho't of the words of the Master,
  That they in that pathway are few,
But I watched in the way they were going,
  It leadeth straight up to the throne—
To the humble, the righteous, the simple,
  Its portals are open alone.

For an Album.

WE WILL stop in the morn of life's journey,
    Will stop on the restless seashore,
And gather up pearls of remembrance,
    As treasures to keep evermore.

The gold of the miser will perish,
    The blade of the warrior will rust,
The hearts of the fairest will sicken,
    And dust will return unto dust.

But the tokens that friendship has given,
    By a word or the glance of the eye,
Will enter the portals of Heaven,
    Will brighten our crowns in the sky.

✿✿✿

Now the Land of Peace Provides.

Now the land of peace provides
    Sweeter rest than all besides;
    Heaven's glories be with thee
    Lasting as Eternity.

Bravely do and firmly fight
    In the cause of all that's right;
    Then will thy glories be
    Lasting as Eternity.

All the best of wishes send
   I to you, as to a friend;
May your sheaves full many be
   For the blest Eternity.

❧❧❧

Elgeroη.

THE bright sun now is gleaming,
  The spring birds now are singing,
And sweetly forth is streaming
    The brooklet from the glen.
All things with beauty laden,
As well the youth and maiden,
It seems as fair as Aiden,
    This habitat of men.

The deep blue sea is roaring,
The tidal wave is pouring,
The little sprays are soaring,
    When on the rocks they burst;
And I extol their beauty,
I know it is my duty,
For wide as their repute be,
    I praise them tho' not first.

The blue sky ne'er was clearer,
And friendship ne'er was nearer,
And beauty ne'er was dearer
    Than they are to me now.
All nature ne'er was brighter,

My heart was never lighter,
Or heartstrings ever tighter
    In harmony, I trow.

While these are quite a treasure,
Their beauty beyond measure,
Affording greatest pleasure
    To those beneath the sun;
Yet song bird free, or maiden,
Or angel fair, of Aiden,
Are not with beauty laden
    As fairy Elgeron.

But I cannot portray it,
By figures ne'er array it,
The sweetest purest lay, it
    Never gives the sum.
Thy song no bird outcarols,
Thy voice beyond the seraphs,
My angels crown with laurels,
    Our beauty, Elgeron.

✼✼✼

Lines to a Lady

ON HER TWENTY-FIRST BIRTHDAY.

TWENTY-ONE. The years have flown
    Since first God granted life to thee,
And made that mortal vessel hold
    A soul to meet Eternity.

When first the light upon thine eyes
 Had cast an ether tint of blue,
It seemed a form from Paradise,
 With all of that celestial hue.

Thy soul was free and knew no care,
 Thy smiles came from thy very heart;
No surface smiles were needed there
 To cover wounds of sorrow's darts.

But twenty-one. I shall not say
 What care and toil have wrought thee now;
What sad reflections grieve thy way,
 What sorrows furrow thy fair brow.

What of the past upon thy way?
 Have flowers sought to give thee joy,
And mingle fragrance with thy lay,
 To cast away thy heart's alloy?

Or have thy steps misguided been?
 Deception with his baneful wail,
Has sought thee out a tear drop stain,
 And lured thee on with that deigned smile?

But such is life. Our purest joy
 Is never of deception free;
Our fondest hopes all idle toys,
 Save those for all Eternity.

Sure all thy gifts are solemn things,
 And now I in that pathway plod;
But mark thy years on Time's fleet wings
 For twenty-one have gone to God.

You and I, Little Boy.

IF YOU and I, little boy, were birds,
And had little wings to fly unheard,
  We would soar away to the highest tree,
  And sing and sing in our merriest glee,
If you and I, little boy, were birds.

But you and I, little boy, are not,
High Heaven makes it a sadder lot;
  Our whole long life may be a moan,
  May be laughs of joy, but anon the groan,
And you and I, little boy, are not.

Yet you and I, little boy, may be,
When time has gone, and eternity
  Will give us wings, sweet voices, too,
  Will give us rest with the saints so true,
Then you and I, little boy, may be.

✿✿✿.

The Scholar's Mission.

RODRY CERYL, reared upon the plain,
Tho'tless boy days passed with scarce a pain;
Rain and sunshine nurtured Heaven's plan,
Until the boy had grown to be a man.

A modest mansion was his dwelling place
His father built when with another race,
But they were gone, and peopled was the plain
With fairer maidens and with fairer swains.

Now Rodry loved his early schoolboy days,
And lingered oft upon their pleasant ways;
The pretty faces that he used to see,
Some, fairer grown, were in eternity.

And some upon the neighboring hilltops dwell,
Where warbling notes from shady branches swell,
And some afar in distant countries roam
To meet no more save in their final home.

With romping boys he used to roam the plain,
On school grounds play the loved and vig'rous game
And misdemeanors sometimes led astray,
In loving less the study than the play.

His mother died while Rodry yet was young,
A precious jewel thus from him was wrung,
And many an hour among her garden plots,
He sat and viewed the bright forget-me-nots.

Four locust trees gave forth their leaves in spring
Before the door and near the purling stream,
The father placed when Rodry's mother died,
As trust in Him who had been crucified.

And 'neath a tree a slab constructed seat,
Where May time brought a perfume strangely sweet,
The father used to sit with Rodry there,
And saintly talk or say his evening prayer.

Tho' he had lands and title for his son,
To whom to give when he his work had done;

Yet like a wise, a prudent, thoughtful sage,
He gave to him a better heritage.

'Twas never written as a document,
No lawyer's fee for such a service spent;
But firmly put from which to never part,
On spirit tablets of a spirit heart.

The father first a good example laid,
And paid his dues as he declared them paid,
And somewhat power was given to him there,
By godly doings and by godly prayer.

Experience gained in long and earnest years,
With watchfulness and anxiousness and fears,
Had taught him much by premises ne'er given,
That bettered earth, approximated Heaven,

Now Rodry longed to delve in classic lore;
The district school at which he used to pore
O'er book intent, had now insipid grown
For want of that beyond the present known.

The stately college reared in distant view,
An emblem of what in its chambers grew,
And which transplanted with a master hand,
Went in the world to edify the land.

So Rodry's wants could there be satisfied,
The starving mind no healthful food denied.
When this was learned, straightway was sent to
      school,
To gather power or be a classic fool.

But yet the father had some ground for fear,
Some dangers, too, were ever lurking near;
While knowing well his son was bold and strong,
Hell's emissaries might lead him in the wrong.

One autumn eve just ere he went away,
Beneath the trees, when eve was growing gray,
The selfsame seat, on which in years agone
They used to sit, this eve they sat alone.

The huge, dull clouds hung heavy in the west,
White silver fringings flitted from their crest,
And stately rose, bringing good or will,
And strove away the mighty dome to fill.

Across the eastern heath the moon arose
And smiled upon the world in calm repose;
But on the heath, just at its surface there,
Lingered awhile as if in evening prayer.

And zephyrs played among the locust trees
A murmuring tune, as if on calmer seas,
And lulled so solemn, the patriarch's silent prayer
Brought earnest tho't to younger Rodry there.

But silent, he was thinking of the day,
Which now was come and calling him away;
'Twas duty's voice, and ever and anon
Asked sacrifice for what its course had won.

He now would leave his boyhood haunts for aye,
The olden shades that cheered him many a day,
The orchard trees 'neath which we used to roam,
And all the dear environments of home.

He tho't of words his mother used to say,
When e'en a child she cheered him at his play,
And all the pathos of those words were there,
And all the power of the early prayer.

Integrity had marked his early years,
When sinning 'twas thro' weakness or thro' fears,

And penance given had solace in the bow,
For cleared away the clouds that grieved him so.

It is not all a sadness to muse thus,
When duty calls, tho' solemn 'tis to us;
Yet joy wells forth to know we're in the right,
And quickens strength to conquer in the fight.

Some crystal tears gushed from his youthful eyes,
A swelling sigh responsively did rise;
A battle fought, had gaind a victory,
Resolved to stand, bound by no slavery.

Some noble tho'ts as these ran through his brain,
And some to follow quickly in this train
Were called to halt when Rodry's father said,
As waking from a seeming dream he had:

"My boy, to-night may end our meeting here,
Each summer time we met till autumn sear,
And gathered crumbs of wisdom and of power,
By meeting often in the twilight hour.

"To-night my eyes look o'er those scenes again,
And catch some sweetness of those meetings then;
Thou knowest well the path that thou shouldst go,
But some would lead thee in the path of woe.

"So now, my boy, this last behest I make
For right and truth, and for thy mother's sake,
Thou art called to go upon a mission grand,
Thy lot improve to elevate the land.

"Remember this, thou workst not for thyself,
For fame alone, or for entrancing pelf,
Thine is a work not bounded by the seas,
Nor Heaven above, nor where the angels breathe.

"So close thy heart against each sinful hour,
And learn thy tasks, 'twill generate thee power.
And what thou dost do not for wealth or praise,
Deceitful tongues regard not wisdom's ways.

"Let all thy ends be for thy neighbor's good,
Tho' he reside from thee full many a rood;
What is thy neighbor's is thy country's, too,
What thy country's, claims the whole world thro'.

"To serve thy God thou servest thy fellow men,
To laud his name thou elevatest them,
What grievest Him doth cast thy neighbor down,
Deludeth thee and draweth clouds around.

"So then when thou art called a scholar, boy,
Thy power's extent will be no idle toy;
Stand at the helm with calm, unerring hand,
Steer thro' the wave toward the glory land."

♪♪♪

The Sunbeam.

ONE early morn I wandered lonely forth,
　　O'er hill and wold and glen;
　　　The farm boy's merry strain
　　　Rang out the hills again;
　　　And in the brooklet main
The eddying streamlet bubbled brightly forth.

The merry bird that soared so high aloft,
　　　Or sang within the trees
　　　That nodded with the breeze,

Seemed glad with things like these,
And eyed me, greatly pleased
That I should list at song so sweet and soft.

And then I threw me gayly on the earth,
Where green the grasses grew,
And many a fragrance threw
To mingle with the dew,
Which sipped the sweet cuckoo,
And gave it in her pretty song of mirth.

And while I lay there dreaming all alone,
Out from the eastern hill,
While all the birds did fill
The trees, the mead, the rill
With carol and with trill,
A single ray of golden beauty shone.

A single ray of golden, beautied light,
That filled my heart with glee
To know it shone on me;
But then there rose a sea
Of trouble suddenly,
Must send a pension to its fountain height.

❧❧❧